TOP OF THE WORLD

A SUMMIT SPRINGS NOVEL

JODI PAYNE

This is a work of fiction. Names, characters, places, and incidents either are the product of the author's imagination or are used fictitiously. Any resemblance to actual events, locales, organizations, or persons, living or dead, is entirely coincidental and beyond the intent of either the author or the publisher.

To BA and Julia, who offered me my first opportunity to publish sapphic romance and now, a million years later, offered me this opportunity too.

And to my wife, who constantly has to repeat herself because I'm writing and not listening.

Much love and appreciation.

CHAPTER 1

Frankie braked to a stop in the parking lot at the bottom of the bike trail and shared a high five with the pair she'd joined up with at the top of the mountain. "Whoo! That was sweet." She tugged her helmet off and ran her fingers over her blond braid, grinning with the adrenaline rush of a great ride.

"Right? You kicked ass. That slalom bit toward the end is pretty gnarly, huh? You gotta watch that last bend...the one with the boulder on the outside." Patrick and Heather were experienced and pretty hardcore on the trail. Frankie wasn't sure if they were locals or just came up here a lot, but they were serious terrain riders and had shown her all the best places to trick or get some air along the way. They'd been good people to run into.

"Totally." She nodded, still breathing hard from the workout. "I'm glad you were in front of me, man. The only reason I didn't bite it is because you almost did."

They all laughed. Frankie went for her water bottle and took a big swig, washing the dust from the last bit of trail out of her mouth.

"Are you from around here?" Heather got off her bike and started stretching.

"No. I'm a seasonal hire up at Marmot and Moose." She was pretty stoked about it too.

"The outfitters? Oh, dude. Awesome. Are you a guide? I didn't know they were into biking."

"They are this year." She gave Heather a wink. "They hired me to set up the program and run it as a trial thing for the summer." And if it worked out, she'd find a way to be useful over the winter too. It paid well, better than anything she'd done before, and she loved biking. "We'll see how it goes."

"Well, I hope it goes well."

"Thanks." Frankie did too. The job had been hard to land —she'd had two interviews with Liz and Lupe and still hadn't been officially hired until she'd made it out here and they'd met her in person. She got it, they were putting a lot of trust in her. Mountain biking was a new venture for the M&M this summer, and she knew they wanted to do it right.

All she had to do now was not fuck it up. That wasn't an option. She needed the job, sure, and it was a good one, but she hadn't actually come all the way out here for the work.

She'd come out here for Aspen.

Aspen Young—her Penny.

Named for the tree, not the town.

Patrick opened the back of a black pickup and started loading their gear. Heather pulled out her phone. "Take my number in case you're looking for someone to ride with. Riding alone up here's not a great idea; you were smart to wait for someone to hook up with."

She knew. She'd made that mistake once; she wasn't going to make it again. "Thank you. That would be awesome." She handed Heather her phone and Heather put in her info. "Heather Booth. Got it."

"Booth for now. Patrick's last name is Young. We got married a month ago, and I still haven't decided yet if I'm taking his name or keeping my own. It's making him crazy."

"Patrick Young?" *Holy shit.* It couldn't be. She wasn't ever that lucky. "And you all are local?"

"Patrick has a house just outside of town. We love it. I'm a teacher and Patrick does ski patrol. He's got family here too, so there's even more reason to stay."

"Oh…very cool."

No fucking way.

Patrick turned around, and suddenly Frankie could see the resemblance. She'd missed it when he was wearing his helmet. Patrick and Penny had the same dark eyes, the same wide smile. He had to be the little brother she'd talked about.

Whoa.

"You got Heather's number, right? Let's do this again. We can hook you up with some other riders too." Patrick stuck out his hand and she shook it.

"Thanks. It was great to meet you both."

Say hi to your sister for me.

Yeah, no. Not yet.

Heather put her bike on the rack, and it looked like they were all packed up. "Good luck with M and M; they're great people."

"Thank you. Fingers crossed." Frankie got out of the way so Patrick could pull his truck out, and gave them a wave as they drove away.

Okay, that was totally wild.

Not only had she just had an awesome ride, but of all people, she'd actually run into Penny's brother on the trail. For a second, she'd considered telling Patrick she knew Penny, but she didn't want Penny to hear she was in town from anyone but her.

She didn't think it was going to go over so well.

She walked her bike to her Forester and set it on the rack, then tossed all her gear onto the back seat. Waiting for her on the passenger seat was a Luna Bar and a bottle of water, and she opened both. She was hungry after that ride. Maybe she'd head into town to scope out some food. Or maybe she'd see if she could figure out where Penny had landed when she moved home again.

But as soon as the Luna Bar hit her stomach, she realized there was no way she was going to make it into town today. She was still adjusting to the altitude, and it was hitting her hard after that ride. Burlington was a whopping two hundred feet above sea level. Mount Mansfield was as high as she'd ever been until now at forty-three hundred feet, and she'd only spent a few hours at a time up there. This was her second day in Summit Springs at nearly six thousand feet flat, and she was feeling it.

Like, whoa.

She'd taken ibuprofen this morning but her headache was returning fast, and this time she was feeling pretty nauseated too. She'd obviously pushed too hard too soon. What she needed now was more water and some rest, or she was going to regret that ride.

She wanted to explore, but that was just not happening. Maybe tomorrow. For now, it was back to the bunkhouse for a nap.

CHAPTER 2

One of the best things about summer in Summit Springs was the sunset. Aspen loved that the days were finally getting longer and she could sit on the back deck with a glass of wine after dinner and watch the sun disappear behind the mountains in an explosion of orange and pink, or red and purple, whatever colors Mother Nature had on her mind.

That was her plan for tonight, after her wilted spinach and steak salad, which she was already salivating over as she locked up her art gallery for the day.

The other great thing about summer was the tourists. Sales were usually good in the winter, when skiing and snowboarding were big up at Pines Peak. In the summer when everything outdoors was possible, they were typically even better. But spring was unpredictable. In the spring the snow was melting, and the weather wasn't warm enough yet for most people to spend a lot of time outdoors, but it often wasn't cold enough to make snow either. The hiking and biking trails were still too muddy to use safely. Spring didn't draw the visitors the way summer was about to. And tourists meant sales. This spring had been a tough one for her co-op of artists, and last month she'd barely gotten the business bills paid.

And the rent on the shop and the studio space was late for June.

Hers wasn't the only business feeling it. She understood now why some people had been so upset when the resort's expansion plans had been in the works. She'd arrived home to Summit Springs just in time to cast her vote on a local resolution that was meant to limit the new program. It had failed by quite a margin. It was a double-edged sword: The new programs created many more year-round jobs, but the resort's new all-inclusive winter skiing packages kept people on the resort grounds for everything—including their meals and their shopping.

Still, she had high hopes for summer. *Soon*, she told herself. *Soon they'd all be making some money again.* She'd be staffing the gallery in the evenings to accommodate downtown shoppers, diners, and ice cream buyers. They just needed to make it through the month.

Tonight, though, she planned to enjoy her salad and watch the sun set.

Her brother's car was there when she pulled into the driveway, and she sighed. She loved Patrick, and his girlfrie —*wife* was very sweet, but that didn't stop her from wishing she had the house to herself sometimes. Sharing the big house they'd grown up in was the price she had to pay for their amazing view, the relative privacy, and the complete lack of mortgage. It was more than worth it, and neither she nor Patrick could even think of selling.

Besides, it was big enough that they could more or less live at opposite ends of the house, and just share the big fire-place in the living room and the kitchen, and since she did most of the cooking, there was hope for a quiet kitchen tonight at least.

She went inside and hung up her jacket—another thing she loved was that summertime didn't always mean warmth at night—dropped her keys in the bowl by the door, then went nosing around to see what was what and who was where.

She didn't find anyone, and the kitchen was quiet.

Maybe the newlyweds were napping.

And that was all she needed to suppose about that.

Ew.

She shook her head at herself and went to change, trading her skirt and boots for sweats and flip-flops, and tugged on a hoodie. On her way back to the kitchen she stopped by the little bar in the den and poured herself a glass of wine, then took her glass and the rest of the bottle with her.

She was spoiled living here, she knew that, and she did her best to appreciate it.

Aspen pulled the steak she'd been marinating all day from the fridge, took it out to the gas grill, and threw it on. It was a big one, big enough for all of them. Deep down she knew the scent of sizzling beef would bring her brother running, so she wasn't shocked at all when he showed up.

"What's for dinner?"

She looked at the steak, then at him. "Really?"

"I mean what *else* is for dinner?" Patrick rubbed his neck sheepishly. He was too adorable to be mad at.

"I'm making a spinach salad with steak. There's enough here for you and Heather if you're hungry." She snorted. "And I know you're hungry."

"I'm always hungry."

She noted Patrick's sleepy look. His wavy hair was mussed on top, dark curls going every which way. "Is Heather still in bed?"

"Yeah, we—"

She raised a hand to stop him. "Nope. That's enough information, thank you."

"I was going to say, *sister*, that we spent the morning rocking a trail up on the mountain."

"So one trail ride wipes you out, now, little brother?" She laughed. "Please."

"No..." Patrick grinned smugly. "There's more to the story, but you said you didn't want to know."

"Exactly right." Aspen sipped her wine.

"Did you have a good day?"

"I did. The gallery wasn't busy, but a couple of people were buying. I sold two pottery pieces to a woman who was out here with her husband from Denver for the weekend."

"Yours?"

"A vase of mine, and one of Minnie's leaf platters." The woman had bought the platter as a gift but the vase for herself, which made Aspen happy.

She poked at the steak, deciding it needed another minute before she turned it over, and waited for Patrick to chime in.

"I like it rare, but Heather likes hers medium."

So predictable.

If there was cooking happening in the house, she was the one doing it. She knew how everyone liked everything, just like Mom used to. "I know. Medium-well." She usually pulled the steak off and carved it, then put a small end chunk in cast iron on the stovetop to cook Heather's the rest of the way. Personally, she thought well-done beef was a crime, but she kept that to herself. "Do you want salads?"

"Would you please make us some potatoes?"

One thing she had to say for her brother: He might be an opportunist, but he was always polite. *Look at that, Mom. You raised him right.* "I can throw a couple of potatoes in for you, sure. You want some spinach too?"

"That would be great." Patrick pointed to her wine. "I'm going to get a beer."

"Sounds good." *I'll let you know when dinner is ready*, she thought, as she watched him go. She flipped the steak, smiling at the loud sizzle and the perfect grill marks on the first side. While that was finishing up, she went back in to put the russets in the microwave. She added one in for herself too; she could do something with it for lunch tomorrow.

At the perfect temperature for medium rare, Aspen pulled the steak off the grill and put it on a large cutting board with a well for the juices. She could hear her father's voice as she set the steak out to rest on the kitchen counter, reminding her that the juices needed to redistribute before she sliced into it. That was another thing she loved about Summit Springs in the summer—remembering all the time she'd spent with Dad when school was out.

Patrick was always telling her to quit living in the past, but she wasn't. They were good memories, fond ones, and she liked living among them. Did she need to get out more? Probably. But she was happy with things as they were.

She gently wilted the spinach and cooked up one end of the steak for Heather. "Dinner!" she shouted and heard Patrick's bedroom door open a second later.

"He's coming. He grabbed a beer and jumped in the shower."

Heather always looked good. She was blessed with that naturally messy thing, with super curly hair that did mostly what it wanted to, and a body that wore clothing easily. She had a great smile too, and was really sweet...Aspen absolutely understood what Patrick saw in her. She tried not to be jealous that he was so happy.

"I prefer him clean." She winked at Heather.

"Me too. Thanks for making dinner."

Aspen shrugged. "It's no problem, I was grilling anyway." She appreciated the thank-you, though.

"Did Patrick tell you we had a great ride today?"

"He mentioned you'd been out."

"It was a perfect day. Wide-open blue sky, lots of sun, and the trail was pretty dry. Good stuff."

Aspen hadn't ridden since high school, so she didn't really know good from bad, except that dry was always better than muddy. "Cool." She resisted the urge to ask if either of them had a job for the summer. Patrick was a ski instructor in the winter months and usually picked up maintenance work on the mountain in the summertime. Heather was an elementary school teacher and had the summer off, but she had no idea if Heather usually found work in those free months or not.

"Patrick said there were potatoes?"

"They're just finishing in the microwave. I know, they're better in the oven, but they take an hour, and Patrick just asked me twenty minutes ago."

"Oh, that's fine. No worries." Heather grabbed plates and Aspen made her spinach salad. Heather took the potatoes out when they were ready. Patrick showed up eventually, barefoot and wearing only a pair of sweat pants.

"Go put a shirt on," she and Heather said at the same time.

Heather even pointed toward the bedroom for emphasis.

"Wow. Damn. Okay, ladies." Patrick laughed, then turned right around and went back down the hall.

Aspen nodded approvingly. "I do like you, Heather. Our parents would have too."

Heather's face lit up. "You think so? I wish I'd met them."

Dad had been gone since her senior year of high school, but Heather had just missed meeting Mom. She and Patrick met right after Mom's funeral. "Wander the house a little and pay attention. You'll get to know them." Bits of her parents were everywhere.

"Aw. I love that. I will."

"One shirt." Patrick breezed back in and kissed Heather's cheek. "Smells good."

Heather pointed to Aspen. "Don't look at me, I'm just eating."

"Thanks for dinner, sis."

"Mhm. How about you buy groceries this weekend? The list is on the fridge." Was that subtle enough?

Patrick was suddenly very interested in his steak. "Yeah. Let me check the old bank account."

"I can do it," Heather offered. "We can, I mean. No problem."

She glanced between them and nodded. "Thanks." Heather might be sorry if she let Patrick get away with that all summer. Then again, Heather was now living rent-free, so maybe it wasn't such a hardship for her after all.

"See? We'll shop. You need to get out and have some fun, Aspen."

It was a good thing she loved the asshole. "Yeah? And you need to start paying some of the bills around here, Patrick." Her brother pitched in when work was steady for him and a lot less when he was between seasonal jobs. She'd been covering most of the bills since she'd moved home again, which was one thing when it was just the two of them, but with Heather moving in, they needed to make a new arrangement.

Patrick opened his mouth, but Heather's hand landed on his shoulder and he shut it quickly.

"Maybe you and I can sit down and talk about the bills, now that I'm living here, you know? Work out a plan?"

Oh-ho. So that's how it is, hm? She wanted to laugh. Was her brother a kept man now? "Sounds great. Coffee on the deck this weekend?"

"Perfect."

"You married a good one, Patrick. I hope you treat her well." That was a joke, of course. He treated Heather very well as far as she could see.

"I did, right? And I treat her great."

Heather shot him a grin. "Oh, you think so, do you?"

God, they were perfect for each other. Aspen had been ready to have it out with her brother before Heather moved in a couple of weeks ago, and now he was mostly out of her hair, and someone else was going grocery shopping.

That was great, right? But why did that also make her feel so…lonely?

She'd been alone for a while without feeling lonely. It was probably just the newlywed thing and how stupid happy they seemed. She just needed to get used to it.

"I'm going to go sit on the deck and eat dinner. You're welcome to join me, I just—"

"Want to watch the sun go down. Like every night."

"Yes. So? If you roll your eyes any harder, Patrick, you're going to hurt yourself."

"Enjoy, Aspen. I'll keep Grumpy off the deck."

Patrick snorted. "Grumpy?"

Aspen picked up her wine and her plate and went outside, a big breath of mountain air making her feel better. She sat at the table and dug into her salad.

She couldn't feel that lonely out here, right? Not with the mountains and the birds and Mother Nature for company.

CHAPTER 3

"*C*offee's ready!"

Frankie groaned and sat up, squinting as a beam of bright sunlight caught her in the eyes. M&M had nice bunkhouses, a big draw for someone like her who didn't have anywhere else to stay, but maybe she should have chosen a bottom bunk. It would have been easier to hide from the daylight down there. The call for coffee woke her up, but whoever it was in the kitchen was singing an overly enthusiastic version of "You Are My Sunshine" that made her want to hide under her pillow again.

"Is that Milo?"

"That is totally Milo."

"Please tell me he doesn't do that every—"

"Yep." She heard laughter from the bunk below. "Every morning. Unless it's not sunny." Alex stood, pulling on a hoodie.

"Yeah, then it's 'Singin' in the Rain.' " Lucy grinned at her from her top bunk across the room. "But hey, the woodstove is always stoked and the coffee's on."

Frankie grinned back at Lucy. "Okay, you sold me."

"Could be worse. Last summer we had Toby."

"Oh, God. Toby."

Frankie climbed out of bed and found slippers and a hoodie of her own. Colorado was even colder than Vermont first thing in the morning. "Toby?"

It was still early in the season, but this bunkhouse was full. A couple of people were in the one next door too, and she'd been told they would all be filling up very soon.

"Toby would wake everyone up to random music on his phone. Bad music."

"Opera."

"Broadway musicals."

"Nickelback." Lucy and Alex cracked up.

"Hey, now. I like Nickelback." Milo had four mugs out on a wobbly table and was filling them each with coffee.

"Me too." She gave Milo a wink.

"Miley Cyrus." Alex reached for a mug.

She cracked up as she shuffled to the little fridge for cream. "Oh. Okay. He's so fired."

"Fired."

"Canceled."

"Sugar?" Milo set a bowl down and Lucy dug into it with a spoon.

"So, what's the plan today?" Frankie asked, putting cream in her coffee and pulling up a chair.

"I've got a hike at eight." Alex scrubbed a hand through their curly hair, trying to tame it. "Kids, I think, high schoolers."

She nodded. "That sounds like fun."

"Oh, I'm so sorry," Lucy said at the same time, making Alex shake their head.

"Yep. You both have it about right."

"I have to saddle up four horses for Liz this morning."

"Is she taking a group out?"

"I'm not sure if she is or if Rhianna's on this morning, but Liz booked it."

"I like her," Frankie chimed in, not sure why that seemed important to her sleepy morning brain.

"She's awesome. Lupe too. You have any issues, Lupe is like…I don't know. Mama bear. She'll fix it."

"Yeah? Good to know. Thanks." She was going to like this place.

She already liked this place.

"You don't start today, do you?" Milo asked, pouring himself more coffee.

"No, I'm here a week early to ride the trails and learn my way around." She wanted to get into town today to meet the folks they were leasing the bikes and equipment from.

"I'm signing up. I love to ride."

"Yeah? I was thinking about taking a group of us up, letting you all play guests and help me figure out where problems might happen."

"I'm in." Everyone said at once, and she grinned wide.

"You all are the best."

"Okay. Let's hop to it, y'all." Milo made a shooing motion.

"How are you so perky in the morning?"

"How are you not?" Milo winked at her and finished his refrain from earlier.

Milo's energy and Lucy's humor were kind of contagious. So was Alex's get-it-done attitude. These were great people, and she could only assume there were more great people coming.

They dressed and talked and scrambled eggs for breakfast wraps for the road, and by seven o'clock, they were all going their separate ways. It was a gorgeous morning, the sun was out, the sky was wide open and deep blue, and Frankie felt… good. Finally. She didn't have anywhere to be this early; she'd planned to check out a flat trail after lunch instead of a downhill route today, taking it easy after yesterday's ride. She'd been so excited to get out there, it had been one of the best days ever, but she'd crashed afterward, napping into the evening. Even then she'd still woken up with a slight headache. The altitude adjustment thing was tougher than she'd expected, and she'd really overdone it.

This morning, though, she was feeling like Frankie again. So today she'd drink another ton of water and go easy on herself; tomorrow she could get back at it.

She wandered out to her car as she ate her breakfast, nodding to some staff members she didn't know yet and by the time she slid into the driver's seat, she had the beginnings of a plan for her day.

Scratchin' Gravel Bike Rental and Repair opened early as she'd hoped it would, and Isley Forrester, the owner, was there and ready to talk. The shop was pretty busy, even at that hour, with people getting geared up for a day on the trails. She wandered along the row of bikes against the front wall, one after another lined up on the floor, and even more hanging above on racks. On the other side of a wide aisle, she found a wall of helmets and other accessories. Lights and reflective vests, kickstands and gear racks. Water bottles. Maps. Snacks.

She loved a bike shop. She knew her way around all of this gear and no matter what shop she was in, they always felt like home.

She spent a good hour talking with Isley about how the leasing contract with M&M worked. They went over what the procedure would be for getting the bikes, maintaining them, borrowing and returning equipment. The shop's parking lot out back was right next to the river and the trail that ran along it. It was a great location, especially for the low-key trail rides, and a better jumping-off point for some of the rides than starting up at the M&M, so Frankie arranged to meet her clients in the gravel lot right next door. Isley and their staff would be there to help outfit everyone with at least a bike and a helmet, and sometimes more serious gear like chest armor depending on the kind of ride. If needed, M&M had a big van and a utility trailer Frankie could use to transport everyone to the base of whatever trail they were going to ride that day.

"This was the easy part, believe it or not," Isley said as they stepped out into the parking lot. "People-wrangling is the tougher part of the job."

"Yeah, I bet. Does the shop do excursions too?"

"Not anymore. That was the point of the partnership with M and M. I have the equipment, but I don't have anywhere for guides to stay, and insurance is expensive. Liz and Lupe have that in place already, you know? When I approached them about it, they jumped right in. This is what they do."

"Well, I'm excited to be working with you." Her outings began in just under a week, when the trails would be a bit drier.

Isley offered a hand and she shook it. "Great to meet you. Come by on Thursday, and we'll check out the bikes and go over the reservations for next week. Our weekends are busy."

"Thanks. Sounds like a plan."

She took one last look around the shop just because, but there was nothing she needed, so she headed back out into the brilliant morning sun with coffee on her mind.

As Frankie sat in the front seat of her car, she realized she actually had no idea where to get coffee. She didn't know anything about this town yet. She could go in and ask Isley, but she liked exploring, so she decided to just head into town and see what she could find.

Downtown Summit Springs seemed even smaller than home. The one main street was a lot like those old west movies with false-front buildings lined up one after the other, shop after shop. How cool was that? She wandered, peering into windows and learning her way around while she tried to find the coffee shop. She passed a barber and a cute bookstore, a little restaurant, a pharmacy, and a jewelry store. She finally saw the sign for "Caffeine Ivy's" and figured she'd finally found what she was looking for. The shop had a small café vibe from the outside, with a glass front, a little menu stand on the sidewalk that said it was "Twofer Tuesday" with coffee and croissant on special, and a cute sign hanging above the front door.

Oh, yeah. This was her kind of place. She wasn't a big drinker, didn't smoke; she didn't have any vices really, except the more caffeine the better. She inhaled deeply as she opened the door to the comforting scent of baked goods and freshly ground coffee. She was definitely feeling better; yesterday all those strong smells would probably have made her turn green. Today, though, it was drawing her in like that snake with the swirly eyes in that Disney movie.

What movie was that? It was right on the tip of her tongue. God, that was going to drive her crazy.

She got in line, surprised that there was one in such a small town, but then again, everyone needed breakfast, right? Or, in her case, second breakfast. That coffee and croissant was calling her name.

"Hey, there." The kid behind the counter was young and adorable and probably would have been in school if it wasn't summertime.

Frankie glanced at his name badge. "Hey, Jake. First question. What's the name of that Disney movie that has the snake with the hypnotic eyes?" She made a swirly gesture in front of her face with her fingers.

"Uh…you mean *Jungle Book*? Ssss…" The kid grinned and sang a line, complete with the snake's hissing "s" sound.

"*Jungle Book*. Yes. Thank you." And now she had an

earworm. *Dammit*. She smiled back. "Can I get a large vanilla latte with an extra shot?"

"Sure. You want the twofer?"

"You know I do." She winked at him and pulled out some cash to put into the tip jar. She only had a couple of bucks, so she stuck her debit card in the reader to pay for her coffee.

"Okay, you're all set. Have a great morning."

"Thank you. You too."

She debated sitting but decided she'd take her snack to go and wander. There wasn't going to be a lot of time for wandering once she officially started work next week. Days off were hers, but days on were long and she expected to be tired. Especially at first. Milo had warned her when she was moving her stuff in that no matter how fit she thought she was now, she wasn't in good enough shape for four to eight hours a day riding trails while looking out for other people. She'd shrugged at first, but after it sank in she realized he was probably right and was glad for the dose of reality so she didn't have to learn that lesson the hard way.

"Uh...*Jungle Book*?" The barista laughed as she read the name on the tall to-go cup, then set it on the counter. She was pretty. Her name tag said "Emily."

Frankie grinned. "Oh. I think maybe that's me."

"That's original."

She pointed to the kid taking orders. "He and I were talking snakes."

"*Oh*. Got it. Hang on, let me get your croissant." Emily put one in a little bakery bag and handed it to her. "Have a great day."

"Thanks. You too." The barista walked away, humming, and Frankie grinned again. They all had the earworm now. She sipped her latte and sighed. *Mmm. Indulgent and perfect.*

She wandered down the street taking bites of her rich, buttery croissant. She passed another restaurant that seemed fun—it was more like a diner, a good place to hang out with some french fries.

When the stores thinned out she turned around, thinking she'd cross the street and take in the shops on that side as she headed back to her car.

"I'm almost there, I can set that up as soon as I get in. What time is he coming by?...Great....Yes, I can be ready by then."

Frankie stepped off the curb as a woman on her cell phone passed her, walking fast. The scent of the woman's perfume made Frankie glance up sharply, suddenly more awake than any cup of coffee could manage.

Penny.

"I'm glad you called. Looking forward to it." Penny continued her phone conversation, completely oblivious to Frankie's presence.

Frankie froze in place just two steps from the sidewalk and watched Penny in her long sweater and tall boots, dark hair flowing out behind her as she hurried across the street. Penny turned left on the sidewalk and Frankie dashed after her, following, but not too close. About halfway up the block, Penny pulled out her keys, opened a door, and disappeared inside.

A sign that read "Pure" hung from an ornate metal hanger. As she got closer, she could read the words below it: "Art Gallery."

Oh. Penny had done it. She was finally running a gallery like she'd talked about.

Good for you, babe.

Penny wouldn't want Frankie to call her right now; the last time they'd seen each other was two years ago, the night before the flight to Denver that Frankie hadn't shown up for. That was going to take more than a surprise hello over morning coffee for Penny to get past. But Frankie was determined to figure this out. Apologize and do things right this time.

She'd made a lot of plans to get out here—finding a job with housing, selling her parents' house back in Vermont, hoping her Subaru would make it out here—but she hadn't given much thought to how this whole "reconcile with Penny" thing was going to go once she got here.

And now she'd found Penny but had no plan.

She didn't get any closer to the gallery. Instead, she sat on a bench a few doors down to finish her coffee and—

And what? Just be near Penny? Be this close and not go in and say hello? She shook her head at herself. Jesus, she wasn't a stalker.

But she sure was acting like one.

CHAPTER 4

*A*spen turned off the alarm and put her bag behind the sales counter. This was a big opportunity for her artists and after her letter, a follow-up email, and several calls, she'd almost written it off as hopeless. If she'd known they'd suddenly be sending someone today, she would have… well, she probably wouldn't have done anything differently other than have more coffee and get to the gallery earlier, but she would have *felt* more ready.

She took a big sip of her coffee and looked around. How ready did she need to be? Everything was spotless, as always, because that was just how she rolled. This gallery was her baby, her creation for herself and the other artists in her co-op. It wasn't flashy or chic or trendy; it was just art. Real art and crafts too, made by talented people who loved what they did. The gallery got them all that much closer to earning a decent living doing it.

This idea she'd come up with to partner with Pines Peak resort was just the next logical step as far as she was concerned.

She went to the front door, made sure it was unlocked,

and turned on the lights. Conifer Street was quiet first thing in the morning this time of year and would stay quiet for another week or two until summer was in full swing. Then Ivy's would have a line out the door with tourists wanting breakfast.

She caught sight of someone sitting on a bench down the block as she turned away. That was unusual, but when she turned back to have another look, they were gone.

Jed Brightlow was parking his truck, though—she saw the Pines Peak logo on the door. It was time to get to work.

She looked into a mosaic mirror hanging on the wall, one of Richie's gorgeous pieces, and checked her hair, then hurried over behind the counter and opened her laptop. Being busy felt like the way to go.

Jed's not doing you a favor. You're adding value, she told herself. People tended to consider artists charity cases. Sure, they always needed more exposure, every artist did, but she wanted to be sure Jed saw she was a businesswoman.

The door opened and Jed came in. He was tall and handsome, had a mustache, and when he dipped his head to say hello, his cowboy hat made the small gesture seem grand. "Good morning."

"Good morning."

"I'm Jed Brightlow, I'm in guest relations up at Pines Peak. Are you Ms. Young?"

She smiled, closed the laptop, and came out from behind the counter. "Call me Aspen." She offered him a hand to shake and he took it.

"Jed. Good to meet you. Thanks for being available on such short notice."

"I was glad to hear you were coming by. I'd first contacted your office in the fall, but I hadn't received a response."

"Oh." Jed looked properly sheepish. "Well, that was rude of me. I'm sorry about that. We get busy going into the winter season, and I didn't have the time to think about something new. I do now, though, and I'm glad you contacted me again."

She understood that; winter was big business here. Still, he could have at least let her know. She gestured farther into the gallery. "Listen, it's great that you're here now. I think we have something to offer you. Can I show you around?"

Jed nodded. "Yes. Sounds good."

They walked through the gallery as they talked, and she was careful to show him the kinds of things she thought would work for the various gift shops on the resort grounds. "I noticed that you've made a point of bringing in some other local merch into your gift shops, and I thought some giftable or unusual items from local artists would go over really well. When I visited in the fall I saw mugs from Ivy's, T-shirts from the diner, I spotted a rack of earrings and necklaces from the jewelry store up the block...and I thought, if you like selling those things, why not—"

"Something made by hand that our guests won't find anywhere else?" Jed repeated her own words, and she blinked, surprised.

"Exactly."

"I read your proposal. The whole thing. It's a great idea, and I don't know why I hadn't thought to approach you myself before now."

Aspen couldn't help her smile or the goose bumps. "It is a good idea, right?"

Jed chuckled. "It is. We have three shops, as I am sure you know. I have a few ideas for the smaller ones, but one of them is high-end. Can you show me some things you think could work well in that one?"

She could do that, and she did. She showed him smaller items that would fit easily into a suitcase and not be too fragile. Pretty things that people could bring home as gifts for family or coworkers. And larger, more expensive items, like Richie's mirror, that folks would more likely buy for themselves. Statement pieces. Artwork to show off.

By the time Jed left, they had a handshake agreement. He told her to expect a contract by email, and she gave him one of their brochures and her business card on his way out.

She stood calmly as the door closed behind him.

This was crazy. It was amazing. It was a random Tuesday morning, and she'd just made her first deal, ever.

She hurried back to her laptop and fired off an email to the co-op members, letting them know she would be putting some of their work out on consignment and she'd have more news during their upcoming meeting. Next, she picked up the phone to call Patrick.

"Hey, there." Patrick had a voice like Dad's, smooth and deep. It made her smile.

"Hey. So I have some really good news and I feel like celebrating."

"No shit? What's your good news?"

"You want to come into town later and get a drink? Maybe dinner? And I'll tell you all about it."

"Oh. Damn. Heather just invited someone over for dinner tonight."

"To our house? Who's cooking?"

"Well, we are. I think."

"Give me that." There was a rustling on the phone; then Heather came on. "You have good news? Come home for dinner and we'll make it a party. We'll cook for you. We'll even spring for the wine. I want to know everything."

That was sweet. "Should I be worried about Patrick in the kitchen?"

"No, because he's not doing anything but getting in my way."

"Hey," Patrick protested. "Is that on speaker now? Good.

Aspen. We'll take you out for a drink this weekend. I can't wait to hear your news. Dinner is about six. Okay?"

"Yeah, we can't wait to hear all about it." Heather said from somewhere farther away this time.

She laughed. "Okay. I will let you cook and meet your friend, and...wait. This isn't some stupid blind date is it?"

"It's just someone we met yesterday on the trail. She's new in town, she rides like a badass, and that's literally all we know about her. I promise."

"Okay. Fine. Good. I'll see you around six."

"Great. Bye."

"Bye, Asp—" Patrick cut Heather off, hanging up the phone. She put hers down and promised herself to hold them to that drink this weekend.

Meanwhile, there were people in her kitchen.

Cooking. Or trying to.

She should have asked what they were making.

CHAPTER 5

*V*ermont had plenty of back roads through the middle of nowhere, even narrow roads leading up mountain passes, but they were different than this. This road was just as winding but wider, more open, and much longer. As she turned yet another rocky, tree-lined corner, Frankie squinted at Google Maps to make sure she was still on the right road. She just seemed to be going higher and deeper into nowhere. According to the map she wasn't lost, though, so she kept on driving uphill.

It was beautiful up here, and occasionally she'd glance over and let herself admire, but mostly she was forcing herself to keep her eyes on the unfamiliar road. Thankfully her Subaru was humming along gamely on the hills. Here and there was a driveway with a mailbox at the end, and she kept hoping the next one would be Patrick and Heather's place.

Patrick, Heather, and *Penny's* place.

Was this an asshole move? Showing up to dinner knowing there was a chance she could run into her ex, but leaving her hosts in the dark? She knew what she was doing.

She knew she might cause a scene and that it might look like she was taking advantage of a new friendship....Okay, she pretty much was taking advantage of a new friendship.

But if she hadn't gotten Patrick's last name she might never have made the connection, and this would have been a total coincidence, right? They would still have invited her, she would still be here...she'd just be clueless.

She sighed as she turned another corner. Right. Okay. She was a dick. She would fess up somehow before this became a mess. She'd...offer to leave or...something.

Maybe Penny wouldn't even be there. Then it would be a moot point, right?

Except she wanted Penny to be there.

Watch the road, figure it out when you get there.

Seriously, if she didn't stop letting her mind wander, she was going to drive herself off one of these curves, and none of this fretting would matter. She rounded another corner and the trees along the side of the road just stopped, opening up to this amazing view of mountain peaks and vast sky, and suddenly the whole crazy drive became completely worth it.

Oh, man. Look at this.

Now she was excited, and she tried to find somewhere to pull over so she could stop and take in the view, but she didn't find one.

She did finally find Patrick and Heather's—and Penny's—driveway.

Whoa.

This was their view? She'd made friends with the right people.

She turned in and drove up the driveway, easily finding somewhere to park. The house was gorgeous; it had a wood exterior with an A-frame roof, tall windows, and a wrap-around deck. There were two cars in the driveway, and she panicked a little. One of them she recognized as Patrick's

Jeep. Was the other one Penny's? Fuck, she was a terrible stalker; she didn't even know what kind of car Penny drove.

She puffed out a breath, reached for the passenger seat, and grabbed the bottle of wine she'd brought with her. She was here now—whatever mistake it might be, she was already in it. Time to suck it up and face the consequences.

She had this.

As she climbed the stairs to the deck, the view drew her in, and before she knocked she wandered over to the deck railing. The mountains seemed just endless from up here, and the sky was higher than the few puffy clouds that clung to their peaks.

Wow.

"You made it."

Frankie jumped at the sound of Heather's voice and turned to face her. "Yes. I—sorry. This view…"

"I know. Isn't it amazing?" Heather leaned on the railing with her.

"I was about to knock, but I got distracted."

"I get it. Patrick walks right by it sometimes. He was raised in this house and he's used to it, I guess." Heather shook her head, and Frankie saw the look of genuine wonder on her face. "But I still can't believe I live here now."

This was the house Penny was born in. This wasn't just any random place. This was the house Penny talked about so much, and the place she'd come home to. She was in Penny's personal space now. She needed to respect that. This was a bad idea.

She needed to come clean.

"Listen, Heather—"

"Come on in, maybe we'll come back and watch the sunset."

"Oh, sure. Uh…I brought wine." She held the bottle out, feeling awkward.

"Hey, that's great. Thank you." Heather took the bottle and led her inside. "Aspen will appreciate that."

Oh, God. Penny. "Heather, I really need to tell you—"

"Hey, Frankie. Welcome." Patrick was washing dishes and nodded to her. "You found the place okay?"

"Oh, yeah. I mean...it's just one road."

"One long, winding road." Heather laughed.

"Right? I kept thinking I had to be lost."

"Sorry about that. I should have warned you. It's a bit of an adventure the first time people come up here." Patrick dried his hands and came over to give her a hug.

"You could have just said it's the driveway after the trees disappear and you can see heaven." She grinned. It had felt just like that. Like angels might have started singing as she turned that corner.

"I don't warn people about that part on purpose," Patrick confessed. "Everyone says the same thing—why ruin the surprise?"

"We're making like a quick, fakey chicken Alfredo. I was just about to put a salad together." Heather set the wine on the counter.

"I can help," she offered. "Pasta is great. I can hardly make chicken by itself, let alone Alfredo."

Patrick glanced at Heather. "Does that get me off the hook?"

"No." Heather sighed. "Nice try. You get to set the table. We're eating on the deck, so turn on the heater, will you?"

"On it. Glad you made it, Frankie."

"Yeah. Um..." Patrick disappeared outside before she could get anything out about Penny.

"Are you okay with peppers in your salad? Some people aren't good with peppers."

"Peppers are fine. Anything is fine. Thanks. Listen, I need to tell you something."

Heather nodded and went to the fridge. "What's up? Are you okay?"

"Yes, I'm fine." She'd finally adjusted to the altitude, now if she could just get this out of her mouth. "It's about Pen —Aspen."

"Have you met Aspen? She'll be here in a bit; she closes up the gallery around six."

"I know her. From Vermont. She and I went to school together and...we...uh. We dated. A bit." A bit? They'd lived in each other's pockets and fucked like bunnies for a summer and two whole semesters.

Heather closed the fridge door and stared at her. "You... and Aspen?"

She nodded, feeling so fucking guilty for lying. Jesus, this was a mess. What was she thinking?

"I should probably...this was a nice invitation...I mean, I had no idea who Patrick was when I met you on the trail; that was total coincidence, but I figured it out after and I should have said something before I accepted for tonight. I just—I didn't want Penny to find out I was here from...from anyone else. I wanted to tell her myself."

"Penny?" Heather's head tilted. "Okay. So it didn't end well, I take it?"

It ended. She hadn't ended it well. "It wasn't like that. We didn't fight or anything. I just—"

Heather held up a hand. "You don't have to tell me. But...I mean, is it going to make dinner awkward?"

Frankie sighed. "I don't know. Maybe. Yes, probably. Maybe I should go? We can do this another time. I don't think I should ambush her in her own house."

"Mm. Yeah. And, well, it's just that she's got something to tell us about when she gets home, something she wants to celebrate..." Heather winced a little. "She was excited, you know?"

Frankie nodded. "Yeah. I get it. You know what? I definitely don't want to ruin her day then. And I don't want you two in the middle of this. I'm so sorry. But we should ride again soon."

"Oh, for sure."

"Cool. So you'll explain to Patrick for me? I'm just—"

The door opened, letting in a cool breeze. "Okay. I'm worried about my kitchen, Patrick."

Penny.

Shit.

Fuck. She didn't get out fast enough. She looked at Heather, who just smiled and shrugged.

Right. It was what it was now, huh? Not much she could do about it. *Made your bed, Frankie...*

"It's fine, sis. I even did the dishes. You're going to be surprised, I promise." Patrick was right behind her.

"You think? Well, it does smell good in—"

Their eyes met as soon as Frankie turned around. Penny stared at her, confused at first. Then her eyes narrowed. Frankie froze, waiting for Penny to yell or throw her out. Anything but just stare. *Fuck.* This was—she was an idiot.

This was not a good idea. A very bad idea.

"Frankie."

She swallowed hard, not sure what that tone meant. Penny was beautiful, though, and the stormy look in her dark eyes only made her hotter. Frankie went for casual in response. "Hey, Penny."

"Aspen."

Goddammit.

"Sorry. Aspen." Yeah, that was going to take some work.

"What a surprise." Penny's tone was dry and flat.

"Wait, you two know each other?" Patrick sounded pleased. "How cool is that?"

Penny shrugged. "Yes, it's quite a coincidence." Penny pinned her with a stare, her heart pounding. She'd nearly forgotten how hot Penny was when she was mad. "It's been a while."

It had been two years. Not that long. Well, okay, they'd been long years, but still only two. "It's so good to see you. You look great." It was worth a shot.

Penny walked right past her. "So, what's for dinner?"

Should I go now? She mouthed at Heather.

Heather threw her hands up.

Damn.

"We're making fettuccini Alfredo with chicken." Patrick seemed completely oblivious to any tension in the room.

"Really? That's not the easiest sauce to make." Penny opened a drawer, pulled out a bottle opener, and reached for the wine Frankie had brought.

There was some kind of irony there, she was sure. Frankie just knew karma was going to come for her. Hard.

"I kind of cheated." Heather took a breath and went to stir the sauce. "I found a recipe online where you use a jarred sauce and doctor it up. It tastes good, though."

"I'm making the chicken. In the oven." Patrick looked proud of himself. "Like real chicken."

God, Patrick was so adorable, the cluelessness was completely forgivable.

Penny nodded. "Real chicken is good. Good wine choice too. One of my favorites." She lifted the glass to her lips but hesitated, lowering it as she turned to give Frankie the hairy eyeball.

She started to say something, but Heather jumped on it. "Thanks!"

Aspen's gaze shifted to Heather with a smile; then she lifted the glass to Heather and took a sip.

And just like that, Heather became Frankie's best friend.

Penny sighed and put her glass down. "So what can I do here?"

"Frankie was just about to make the salad."

No, she couldn't stay now. This was a disaster. Frankie took a step toward Heather. "Actually, I was just thinking I should—"

"Great. I'll help too. Let's make a salad, Frankie."

Frankie blinked. What was going on now?

Heather looked between them. "Okay. Perfect. Yum. Uh, Patrick, is the table done?"

"No, I only just got the heater going when Aspen got home."

Heather took his arm and pulled him out the door. "I'll help. Come on."

Patrick glanced over his shoulder. "I should probably check on the—"

"Aspen can keep an eye on the chicken. Right, Aspen?"

"I can handle this. Thank you, Heather."

Oof. Okay. Frankie sighed and looked at her toes. The subtext in this conversation was the stuff of nightmares.

Patrick and Heather went outside and Penny—Aspen, *fuck*—set out a cutting board. She silently opened the fridge and found cucumber, radishes, carrots, baby spinach, and pulled a knife from the knife block on the counter.

Great. Now *Aspen* was mad, silent, and armed too. It really was a nightmare.

"Shouldn't I get a—"

"No."

"I was just leaving, before you arrived. Honest. Ask Heather."

"Why did you come?"

"I didn't know you'd be here for dinner. I mean, I knew it was possible, but Patrick didn't say when he invited me and I—"

Penny put the knife down. "I don't mean to dinner."

"Oh." She blinked at Penny. "You mean to Colorado?"

Duh, of course she means to Colorado, Frankie. God.

"To Summit Springs, Frankie. Colorado is a big state. Why did you come *here?*"

Didn't Penny know? Was this a trick question? Frankie took a deep breath and…lied. "I got a job?"

"Bullshit."

"No, I actually have a job. M and M hired me to help build out their biking program."

"You just happened to take a job in Summit Springs, Colorado, where I just happen to live, and this was complete coincidence? That's what you want me to believe?"

She gave Penny a sheepish look from under her eyelashes. "Yes?"

Penny raised a disbelieving eyebrow. "So, it has nothing to do with me?"

Well, fuck. Fuckity-fucking-mcfuckstick. Penny had just backed her into a corner. Jesus, Penny was so smart.

"What do you want me to say, Penny?"

"It's Aspen." Penny snorted and shook her head. "You came all this way, got yourself a job so you'd have reason to stay in town, somehow managed to get invited to dinner—*at my house*—all of that without having any idea what I might want you to say?"

She swallowed hard. "I'm sorry?"

"Nope." Penny shook her head, her pretty dark curls flowing around her face. "That's not enough. Pass me the bag of spinach."

Frankie sighed and slid the bag over.

"I know. I don't know what I was thinking. I should go."

"So, tell me. Did you really just happen to run into my brother on the mountain? Because stalker is not a good look on you."

"Oh, Penny—Aspen—I swear. I know it seems ridiculous, but that was a total accident. Lucky for me, yes. Crazy lucky, but completely unplanned. I'd forgotten you had a brother, honestly. I'd even forgotten his name." She wasn't stalking anyone. Quite. Not on purpose anyway.

"Good, because Heather thinks she's made a new friend, and Patrick was impressed with your skills up there, and I don't want to have to tell them you used them just to get close to me."

"Oh, my God. I would never. I wanted to see you, sure. I was working up to it, but I've only been here a few days and the altitude got to me, you know? I wanted to be me again before...before I figured out how to find you. But I wasn't—I would never."

"Okay, okay." Penny nodded, raising a hand to stop her. "I didn't think so, honestly. That seemed a little over the top."

She puffed out a breath, relieved. "I did want to see you. I do. But not like that."

"Good. Okay." Penny crossed her arms. "They went to a lot of effort to make the new girl in town feel welcome, and we're not going to make it weird, so—"

"Heather knows," she interrupted. That was important to say.

"Does she?"

"I'd just told her I knew you, that we'd dated, right before you walked in."

"Good. Then she'll understand."

"Understand what?"

"So, here's how this is going to go. You will stay for dinner."

Okay. That was awkward, but fine. Even good, maybe.

"And then you're going back to your bunk at M and M and staying there."

Wait. What? "Didn't you just say they wanted to be friends?"

Penny's laugh was...off. Weirdly dark. "Oh, no worries. If you can dump me without a word of explanation after more than a year of sleeping together, you can easily walk away from them after one dinner."

Frankie's jaw dropped reflexively and she stared at Penny. She wanted to protest or argue or something, but she couldn't find the words. "Penny—"

There was another rush of air as the door opened, but Frankie didn't feel it. The air in the kitchen had gone way colder than it was outside. Penny didn't say another word as her brother and Heather walked in; she just turned away, grabbed an oven mitt, and checked on the chicken.

"She wouldn't let you help, huh?" Patrick passed behind her and pulled down a few more wineglasses. "Aspen doesn't trust people in her kitchen."

"That's not true. I trust people that have earned it."

Ugh. Touché. Goddammit.

"How's the chicken?"

"It's about done. It looks good, too." Penny gave Patrick a pat on the back. "I can't wait to try it."

Penny looked at Frankie, but she shook her head. That was enough said between them for now.

"So, tell us. What is your good news, Aspen?" Heather picked up the bottle of wine and started pouring for all of them. "What are we celebrating?"

Aspen's demeanor completely changed, a bright smile stretching across her face and chasing the storm from her eyes. "You all might not think it's a big deal, but it is to me."

"Stop it. If it's a big deal to you, we're going to celebrate it." Patrick slid an arm around Penny's shoulders and hugged her. Frankie loved the way Penny dropped her head to Patrick's shoulder for a second. So sweet.

"Okay. Well, the gallery took a hit when the resort went all-inclusive this winter, and I had this idea that since a lot of the tourists are staying up there now and don't even make it into town, it would be cool to get some of our work up into their gift shops, you know? They have three of them."

"Oh, that's a great idea." Heather went to the stove and stirred the sauce.

"Yeah, so I contacted them in the fall, and nobody up there responded at all until out of the blue this morning, the guest relations guy came down to talk to me about it."

"No way, really?"

"Yes, really. I got a phone call that he was on his way, and that was it. He was nice, he loved my idea, and he's going to get me a contract. He wants to carry different kinds of things in each of their gift shops." Penny bounced on her toes. "He seemed curious but skeptical when he walked in, and I sold him on it."

"Hey! That's awesome." Heather ran around the counter and gave Penny a hug.

That was amazing news, but Frankie wasn't surprised. When Penny was passionate about something, she made it happen. "Wow, you're actually doing it. That's so cool." The thought popped out of her mouth as words and her eyes went wide. She had definitely meant to stay out of Penny's business.

Penny glanced at her. "Yep. I said I would, and I did." She didn't look any less proud of herself, but Penny's words took careful aim and hit their target.

And they hurt like hell.

"This calls for more wine." Patrick refilled their already half-full glasses and she picked hers up and took a big gulp.

Aspen had made her point, so Frankie sat through dinner and didn't make things awkward, as requested. She ate Patrick's chicken and drank *Aspen's* favorite wine, and tried to enjoy the amazing sunset from a deck she probably wouldn't ever set foot on again.

This was a mistake. All of it. Thinking she could get Aspen to take her back, taking this job, coming out here…it was a good job and she'd make the best of it, but she'd made a horrible mistake.

It was dark when she left that gorgeous house on the mountain, but she didn't let herself cry until she got down off that goddamn winding road. And, it wasn't until she started crying that she realized she hadn't since the morning the flight that was supposed to kick off her new life with Penny, a flight from Burlington to Denver that she'd been looking forward to for months, had taken off without her on it.

CHAPTER 6

*A*spen stared nervously at the kiln. "You ready?"

"No." Minnie snorted behind her. "Never."

Damon laughed. "This is torture. Just get it over with."

"Rip off the Band-Aid?" Aspen grinned at him and opened the kiln.

"Why does this always have to be so stressful?"

Most of the time, Aspen didn't worry about things in the kiln. Cracking and bad glaze, all kinds of things could go wrong in the firing process; she'd even had a couple of pieces explode over the years. Today she was holding her breath, though. She'd thrown a *saké* bottle and six cups with a special porcelain clay that she didn't use very often and had a reputation for behaving badly if it wasn't just thin enough but not too thin. They'd taken her a long time, and she knew she would get good money for them in the shop. They were on their third firing—she'd been painting glaze upon glaze and adding details with each one. Today she planned to start the detailed lines that would finish the pieces off.

"I'm not looking. No looking until we get it all out of here." She took things out of the kiln and passed them to

Minnie, who then passed them to Damon to set on a long table in the studio. She wanted to look, because Minnie had made the neatest set of dishes, and Damon was working on a huge birdbath, but they had a rule: No one was allowed to have a breakdown until the kiln was empty.

"Nope, not looking," Minnie agreed, passing one of her plates to Damon.

"Ooh. So pretty, Min."

Minnie groaned. "Damon!"

"Sorry. Assembly-line method. I forgot."

"Uh-huh."

Aspen peeked at the *saké* bottle as she passed it to Minnie and what she saw looked good, so she let that hold her over while they got all the pieces on the table and sorted.

"Damon. You look." She shook her head and pointed to her *saké* set.

"Yes, ma'am." Damon picked up her pieces one at a time, looked them over and set them back down.

Minnie's sigh sounded relieved. "One of my plates has a tiny crack, but I made two extra, so I just won't use this one."

"Hey, that's good, Min."

"Girl." Damon clucked his tongue. "You are good to go. This set is gorgeous."

"I am?"

"So good. Is this your last round?"

"Yes. I'm putting in all the blacklining today, then one more fire and they'll be done."

"Oh, neat."

Minnie seemed much more relaxed now and was checking out Damon's heavier pieces. "What are all these for?"

"Oh. Let me show you." Damon arranged all the pieces in a line. "So, this will be the bottom of the base, and then these two are going to sit one on top of the other. I need to finish the water basin to go on top of that, which will be painted to look like the body of a swan, and the waterspout is going to be a swan's head. I'm kind of dreading having to make that, but if I can pull it off, I think it's going to work great."

"Very cool. So much work." There was a reason Minnie liked smaller pieces, and Aspen got it. She'd done a few larger pieces, and they took a kind of patience she found difficult to muster. Not that she wouldn't try it again if she had a reason, it just wasn't ever going to be her thing.

She scrutinized her own pieces, though, and was very pleased with their condition after firing, and also with the way the last round of glaze had settled. They looked kind of like they were covered in blobs of color right now, but once she got the details in, there would be cherry blossoms, bamboo, and panda bears.

From this point, everyone had a different path. Minnie's plates were glazed and done, so she set them out to take some pictures. Damon had a ton of building to do, so he carried his own pieces across the room and found an out-of-the-way corner to work in.

Aspen took all of her cups to her workstation and lined them up on her shelf of in-progress work, deciding to line out the *saké* bottle first and take her inspiration from that for the cups.

First, though, she needed another cup of coffee. She was borderline hungover this morning and wasn't even sure how many glasses of wine she'd had last night. She'd been celebrating, after all. The deal with the ski resort wasn't going to make them rich, but it could turn out to be a big step closer for a lot of the co-op artists toward being able to create art full-time instead of waiting tables or cleaning houses, or any of the other things they did to get the rent paid. It was also leverage she could use on her next ask. Artists like Damon might have a harder time with their trademark pieces in some gift shops, but he was smart and knew how to make a living. He could make some smaller pieces specifically to sell up there.

She could blame the headache on the celebration, but Frankie showing up out of nowhere probably had more to do with it. Frankie. In Summit Springs. In her house. She'd thought she was seeing a ghost when she first walked in. And —*dammit*—Frankie looked good. In great shape like always and pretty tan for early in the summer season. Her ex had even put on jeans and a sweater instead of the athletic wear Frankie used to wear constantly, and her blond hair had been loose around her shoulders instead of up in a ponytail. Less jock and more...

Dammit.

That had caught her off guard, to put it mildly, but she thought she'd handled Frankie's intrusion well enough. She'd finally just said what she wanted to say and shut Frankie down like she should have two years ago. It was empowering, and maybe something to celebrate too, though it had taken a few deep breaths to get there.

Aspen sighed. She needed to stop thinking about Frankie. She didn't care if Frankie stayed in town and kept the job or quit and moved home, as long as she didn't have to see her again. She'd surprised herself with how angry she still was, though angry was a lot better than heartbroken, which was how she'd felt when she'd left Vermont and come home alone. She didn't have any interest in making Frankie feel better about herself for having dumped her with no explanation.

Okay. Whoa.

That was over, she'd moved on, and she wasn't going there anymore.

"Earth to Aspen."

She looked up from her *saké* bottle. "Hm?"

"What were you doing, meditating?" Minnie laughed.

She needed that coffee and got up to put on a pot. "Sorry, I got lost in thought."

"Damon was asking about your brother."

"Oh, sorry. What about him, Damon?"

Damon waved her off. "It's not important, I was just making conversation. I was wondering how he and his new wife were getting on now that she's moved in."

"Oh. Good. He and Heather are really happy, she seems to be spoiling him rotten, so I'm sure he's over the moon." However much she liked to complain about the cooking, they were right for each together. Heather was definitely good for Patrick.

"Is it weird living with them both?"

"You'd think it would be, right? But it's not, actually. Heather and I get along quite well. Patrick and I drive each other nuts in that sibling way, but we're good friends too. We've even started to talk about financial things…"

"If it's still good when the money talks happen, you're golden." Damon nodded. "Trust."

She grinned. "Yeah, it was dicey for a second there. Patrick is out of work at the moment, in between ski-instructor and summer maintenance on the mountain, but Heather is a teacher, did I tell you that? So she understands how to budget for a summer without a paycheck. They even made a nice dinner last night."

"That's great," Minnie brought over a coffee cup. "It's good you can stay in that house together."

That was true for a lot of reasons. Her salary running the co-op and gallery wasn't going to pay tourist-town rent by itself, and although her work did sell, it wasn't like a regular paycheck. The house was paid for, though, so she and Patrick only had to split the taxes, not that those weren't steep in a tourist town.

"I definitely need more coffee."

Minnie squinted at her, grinning. "Too much partying?"

"Oh, yeah. You know me. Party animal."

Damon's laugh rang through the big room. "Oh. Sorry."

"Thanks, Damon. I was just starting to feel good about myself."

The giggle that followed was so worth all the teasing. Damon was just full of joy; she loved that about him.

"Too much wine with dinner, after dinner, before dinner…" She shook her head, and Minnie snorted again.

"It happens."

"My ex showed up last night." *Damn*. She hadn't meant to say that. That was the hangover talking. *Come on coffee…*

"You have an ex?"

She snorted. "Funny."

"Seriously. Who have you dated since you've been out here?"

"You are great for the ego, Minnie."

Minnie laughed. "Girl. You have never talked about romantic stuff."

"Can you blame her?" Damon chimed in from across the room. "Look at you, all over her like she can't get herself a date if she wants one."

"Maybe I'm not a kiss-and-tell kind of girl."

Minnie rolled her eyes. "That doesn't matter. Most other people out here are. The men brag, the women gossip, there's no escaping it."

"I guess I've been lucky." She'd been on a couple of dates, but she hadn't kissed anyone, so no one was telling. That was some kind of luck, but maybe not good luck.

"Uh-huh. I guess you've been celibate." Minnie teased, poking her with her elbow. "So did you tell her to get lost? Or did you plan a make-up *rendezvous*?"

"I told her to get lost. Very lost."

"Where did she show up?"

"At my house for dinner."

"What? Man, that's some balls right there."

"If she had any, I ripped them off last night, so hopefully that's the last I see of her." Hopefully. Except she'd seen Frankie in her dreams, hanging above her, blond hair falling around her face, blue eyes staring into hers.

Damon laughed. "Atta girl. We love you because you are the *boss*."

She glanced over at Damon and gave him a fond smile. "For you? More like a mom."

"That too. *Mhm*. That too." That giggle made her day.

The coffee made that lovely sputtering sound as it finished brewing, and she pulled out the pot and filled Minnie's waiting cup.

"I say mad sex with an ex is better than no sex at all." Minnie gave her a wink, put cream in her coffee, and went back to her station.

"Oooh. Mad sex with an ex. I like that. Mad sex with an ex, mad sex with an ex…" Damon added rhythm to the phrase like he was rapping, and Minnie joined in, singing it in a wandering, lilting voice that was as pretty as it was funny.

Then they all cracked up.

"You two are too much. Minnie, I didn't know you could sing."

"You really do need to get out more. Come down to Whitewater on Thursday nights. Open mic. I sing. You'll know a few other faces too."

"You mean actually go to a bar and pretend I have a social life?" She doctored her coffee and made her way to her work.

"Bring the ex." Damon gave her a toothy grin.

Minnie shook her head. "Heck, no. Meet someone new and give that ex something to be sorry about."

"Now you're talking."

She wondered if Frankie was already sorry. Frankie had come a long way and gone to a lot of effort to have a reason to stay in Summit Springs—she wouldn't have done all that if she didn't regret ending things, would she? But regret wasn't the same as being sorry, and even given the opportunity, Frankie still couldn't let go of her own ego enough to tell her what she wanted to hear.

Not last night and not two years ago either.

Frankie was very good at making herself feel better and calling that right.

Aspen sat and sipped her coffee. "I'll come. Thursday, I mean. I'll come hear you sing and…see what's up."

Minnie cheered. "Yay! I will sing a song just for you."

That sounded flirty, but it wasn't. Minnie was happily married to a tall, handsome man. Aspen talked to him from time to time because he was the co-op's attorney. Damon thought Aspen was a boss? Luke was a force to be reckoned with.

Damon put music on, and they all hunkered down and got to work. She didn't worry about the gallery; Cody was in today and he was great. They all took turns working out there so it was never too much for one person, except maybe her, because she also ran the place and took a small salary. That left lots of time for the artists to work in the studio. She and Damon and Minnie were early birds, but by noon, there would be six or eight people back here, and when she closed up the gallery at six, there would be a full house—the co-op had twelve resident artists right now, and this summer she was going to try to pick up a handful more on short-term contracts to help fund the place.

She tried to keep to a daytime schedule, so she could be available if someone working in the gallery needed her, so her "weekends" were almost always Monday and Tuesday when the gallery was closed, like a lot of the shops in town that counted on tourist business. Starting next week, though, they'd be open later. Seven o'clock on weekdays and nine-ish on Friday and Saturday nights. On a nice weekend night in high summer, they'd stay open until people stopped coming in. It wasn't uncommon to close the gallery at eleven on a Saturday in July.

She was looking forward to those nights. They made their best money in the summer.

She had just finished painting her design onto the *saké* bottle when Patrick texted her.

Heather just told me about Frankie. I am such an asshole. I had no idea. Did she play me? I'm so sorry.

She smiled at the text, because under all the stupid little brother stuff, Patrick was really a sweetheart.

She said running into you was a coincidence. I believe her. She did. It would have been pretty hard for your average jock to engineer running into someone on a spiderweb of mountain trails. But Frankie had confessed that she'd figured out who Patrick was before saying yes to dinner. Aspen decided not to tell Patrick that; it wasn't his fault she'd been ambushed by her ex.

Yeah? Okay, cool. Still sucks.

Dinner was great, though. Thank you. You didn't wreck the kitchen, you may have redeemed yourselves.

And we did the dishes!

That was true. They'd done all the cleanup while she'd finished glass of wine number one-too-many.

But I gave her your cell phone number.

What?

I'm sorry!

She groaned out loud. When the next text came in, she sighed so hard Minnie looked up from her.

Hey. This is Frankie. Don't block me yet.

Aspen rolled her eyes. She wanted to. It was tempting.

She ignored the text for now and answered Patrick instead. *It's okay. How could you know? You two are the best. Next time the drinks are on me. A friend of mine is singing at the tavern on Thursday night.*

I'll check with Heather. Sounds like fun. Sorry again about last night and everything.

It's all good bro. Love you.

She put her phone facedown on her worktable and reached for her *saké* bottle, but when her phone vibrated again, she hesitated. It wasn't Patrick; she'd said "Love you," which usually ended their conversations. He never said it back, heaven forbid, but that was okay, she knew.

It was probably Frankie, so, no, she wasn't going to check for a text.

She sighed and picked up the *saké* bottle, looking her design over, turning it slowly in her fingers, thinking about it, trying to envision the finished product in her mind.

But she was already distracted, so when another text came through the vibration against the table might as well have been an earthquake. She glanced at the phone, fingers itching to pick it up.

She shouldn't, because what if it was Frankie? But what if it was the bank? Or that Amazon package she was waiting for? Or maybe her prescription was ready. Or it could be someone texting her to call out sick.

If it was someone calling out sick, she'd need to know right now, right?

Oh, for fuck's sake, Aspen.

She flipped the phone over to discover there was a text from Amazon.

Ha.

But there was also a text from Frankie, that read, *Coffee? It's 3pm. You know you need coffee.*

God, she so needed coffee. And she should have known Frankie wasn't going to give up.

Why did you ask my brother for my number after I told you not to contact me?

There was a pause before those three little dots popped up letting her know Frankie was typing.

Because I have to have one real talk with you, even if you don't want more.

Well, that wasn't playing fair. How do you say no to that? *Are you stalking me? What next? Are you going to show up at the gallery?*

Do you want me to?

She groaned again.

"Is that the ex?" Minnie asked in a goofy stage whisper.

She nodded. "Yes. And she is still an ex. And she's going to remain one."

Damon whistled. "Hell hath no fury like Aspen when her jaw does…that thing."

"What is my jaw doing?" She really had no idea, but both Minnie and Damon laughed at her. "Shut up."

Don't answer my questions with a question. She liked that reply. It was a nonanswer answer and got her right off the hook.

Okay. I'll ask one then. If I'd said the right thing last night, then what? Would you have forgiven me?

When she didn't answer, Frankie sent more.

What if you gave me another chance to say the right thing?
Please?

I'm sorry about last night.

What would she have done if Frankie had told her what she needed to hear? She honestly didn't know. But somehow that last apology made this a definite no. Even someone she knew she wanted to see again wouldn't get off that easy.

Sorry. In the studio.

Tomorrow?

That question she simply didn't answer. The space between heartbreak and hope felt like a short leap over a deep, dark chasm. It was terrifying. She knew she could make the jump if she wanted to, but part of her also knew that if Frankie wasn't right there on the other side, she'd fall in.

So she'd just make Frankie take the leap instead.

She pulled open a drawer and dropped her phone in it, then closed it tight. She had work to do.

CHAPTER 7

*F*rankie never got an answer to her text. She'd waited all afternoon and reread their whole conversation, and Penny never said whether she was willing to go for coffee. But she hadn't told Frankie to lose her number either.

So Frankie decided it wasn't a no.

And if it wasn't a no, by default it was a yes.

The little voice in the back of her mind told her that no answer meant she was being ignored, and that was pretty much definitely a no, but that was the same voice that had told her not to come out here in the first place. Instead of listening then, she'd taken the job at M&M. She was in this thing up to her throat, so why start listening now?

Heather told her that Penny closed up the gallery around six, so she'd been sitting on the bench she'd found yesterday and watching the door since a quarter after five. She'd dressed again in jeans and a blue sweater she knew Penny liked. Used to like. Might like again.

She was an idiot.

But after her breakdown the other night, she realized that

she was an idiot in love. She'd let something perfect get away when Penny flew home to Colorado without her, and she couldn't just let it go anymore.

She hadn't slept after that dinner party at all, thinking about how she'd ended up here. Two years ago, she'd promised Penny she'd finally come out to her homophobic parents, but she hadn't. She'd been younger then and so torn up, and that broken promise had loomed over her in a way it maybe shouldn't have—in a way it didn't anymore. But at the time...

At the time she'd made the hard decision to stay home and take care of a sick woman that hated everything Frankie was over leaving her mother alone and moving away with a woman who was just the opposite. Penny had loved everything about her that her mother hated—or would have hated if she'd ever known.

The bottom line was that she'd broken her own heart when she broke Penny's, and now she was afraid Penny would never forgive her. Or worse, she was terrified after the other night that even if Penny did forgive her, even if she understood, that Penny wasn't interested anymore.

The door to the gallery finally opened, and Penny came through with keys in her hands and locked up. The evening breeze caught Penny's hair and Frankie remembered what it was like to run her hands through it, what it smelled like when she buried her face in those dark waves.

Frankie found a smile as Penny headed toward her on the sidewalk, but Penny's shoulders sagged and she stopped short.

"Really, Frankie?"

"Hi." It only took her a few quick steps to close the distance between them.

"What are you doing here?"

"Well, you didn't say no."

"I didn't—what didn't I say no to?"

"Coffee."

"I didn't say yes either."

"True, but I figured it was fifty-fifty so…" Frankie shrugged and gave Penny a sheepish grin, and she thought she caught just a hint of amusement at the corner of Penny's pink lips.

"I can't drink coffee at this hour; I'll never get to sleep."

Dammit, she remembered now how Penny was. But that wasn't exactly a no, right? Just a no to coffee. This was like a test she'd be perfectly capable of failing if she didn't know Penny so well. "I'll buy you a glass of wine, then. The tavern is this way, right?" She pointed up the street behind Penny.

"Did nothing I said to you last night sink in?"

"I heard you, but—"

Penny's dark eyes narrowed.

"Do you know what you did to me? Do you have any idea what the plane ride out here, alone, sitting next to your goddamn empty seat did to me?"

"I do know. I know exactly. I broke your heart."

Penny's mouth opened for a second, closed again, and her eyes filled with tears.

"I know because I broke mine too."

Penny swiped at her eyes, and Frankie saw all the hurt in Penny's anger. "Good. I hope it hurt like hell. I hope you curled up in a fucking ball for a week and made yourself sick like I did."

She might have, if she'd been able to. But she didn't say that; she figured she deserved whatever dressing down Penny needed to give her right now. "Penny, I'm so sorry. I'm more than sorry, there aren't words for—"

Penny put a hand in the air to cut her off and pulled a key ring out of her pocket. "Come here."

She followed because Penny said to, and she would give

Penny anything she wanted right now. Any talk was better than no talk at all.

They went back inside the gallery and Penny locked them in. "Okay, Frankie. You want words? How about selfish bitch? Or fucking liar?"

Suddenly it felt like all of Summit Springs ran out of oxygen. She couldn't breathe. Penny might as well have punched her in the gut, and she felt like she deserved it.

"You know, now I'm kind of glad you came out here, so I could finally say those things to your face. And the things I said last night. All the things I've wanted to say since you never showed up at the airport and I left Vermont without you. I can't imagine what I did to deserve being abandoned like that, but I hope to fuck no one ever makes you feel that way."

She shook her head, just shook it over and over as she swallowed hard against the sick feeling in her stomach. "You didn't do anything." Her mind was spinning and tears threatened to cloud her vision. Penny was so mad, her eyes even darker than usual. Frankie remembered that temper, how there was no point in trying to reason with a tornado. You either ran for the cellar or you put yourself at its mercy.

She wasn't going to run. She stared into Penny's eyes and waited, offering whatever Penny wanted. Anything. Everything.

Penny could have slapped her, thrown her out, screamed at her some more, and Frankie would have stood there and taken it because she owed Penny that. Instead, Penny stormed toward her like she had fire at her heels and kissed her. She pushed at Frankie's shoulders and bit at her lips, and Frankie let her. If this was what Penny wanted, she was in. She was so in.

Then the fingers that had been shoving her curled into her shirt and tugged her around. Penny pushed her up against the sales counter, lips still so close she could feel Penny's breath and see the blown pupils in those dark eyes. "This doesn't mean I forgive you."

"Okay." She nodded, breathless and wanting.

They stumbled a few steps before crashing into a door, which Penny unlocked with shaking fingers. Once through the door, Penny tossed the key ring onto a desk, shut the door, and turned the lock again.

That was all the permission Frankie needed. She yanked her blue sweater over her head, dropped it, and helped Penny get hers the rest of the way off too. She was stronger, but Penny was taller, and she easily shifted her kisses to the soft part of Penny's breasts that weren't covered by her pretty push-up bra.

Penny reached behind Frankie and opened the clasp on hers, justifying her decision to get dressed in real clothing today and not just wear her sports bra. Not that she'd thought for one second this was where they'd end up. Wherever here was. An office, maybe.

She moved her fingers around to Penny's back as well and popped open the clasp so easily, as if it had just been waiting for her. A little wiggle of their shoulders and their bras slid between them and hit the floor.

It became a different kind of fight then. Penny pushed her into the door and bent to her nipples, and they grew stiff so quickly it made her gasp. She reached down and hiked up Penny's long skirt and as Penny widened her stance, she pushed her knee between Penny's thighs.

They didn't speak, not even sex talk or the filthy things Penny used to say to make her wild; they just rocked together, breasts rubbing just right, tongues tangling as Penny pushed a hand into her jeans. She was so ready for that touch it was almost embarrassing, and Penny's fingers were wet and slippery as they rubbed across her clit.

She grunted because crying out seemed like more of an admission than she wanted to make at that moment, then returned the favor, sliding her hand along her own thigh until she found the edge of Penny's underwear and pushed her fingers under the elastic.

Penny went still for a second, arching away from her thigh to give her fingers more room and Frankie thought she might just die right there. Penny wanted her. Whatever else they had to work out, they still had this. She pushed her fingers across Penny's sensitive nub and replaced that pressure with her palm as she dipped two fingers inside.

Frankie was sure she heard a whimper, just the slightest hint of need before Penny growled and sank teeth into her shoulder.

She did cry out then, because it hurt just right, and because it sent lightning through her, making her beg with her hips for Penny's fingers to breach her too.

But they didn't.

Penny rode her hand, and those knowing fingers slid across her clit over and over until Penny shivered and gasped, mouth dropping open in a beautiful "O" —*O for orgasm*, she thought. *O for out of this world.*

She rocked into Penny's touch, still begging for more but Penny pulled her hand away.

"No...oh, fuck." She was breathless and her eyes were wide in disbelief.

"You want this? You want what I can give you, Frankie?"

Every part of her was on fire, aching with need. "Yes. Yes, please. Fuck, yes."

Penny nodded. "Work harder."

She stared as Penny bent to pick up her clothing and moved away.

Penny was flushed and was still trying to catch her breath, but there was no smile on her face, no knowing look, nothing Frankie could read at all. Penny dressed, fastening her bra and pulling her blouse on, then disappeared through a door. A bathroom, Frankie realized, when she heard the water running.

She got dressed, the toothy bruise Penny had left her with making her wince as she pulled on her bra. She was still a little hormone-drunk as she pulled on her sweater, moving like a robot.

"Your turn," Penny said, leaving the bathroom and crossing to the desk, no evidence of having just gotten off after angry sex. She didn't even have a hair out of place.

Frankie watched Penny, confused, but still not sure if she was feeling hurt or angry. "I get a turn this time?"

"Ooh." Penny laughed darkly. "That was a good one."

She shook her head and went into the bathroom to clean up.

When she came out, Penny wasn't in the room. It was definitely an office, very obviously Penny's office. She recognized some of the photos on the walls and the UVM Catamounts basketball trophy on the windowsill.

She went through the door into the gallery to find Penny waiting by the front door, looking at her phone. Penny glanced up at her, and she felt her phone buzz in her pocket. That was bad timing.

"Ready to go?"

"Penny—"

"Nope. No explanation. Sorry."

"But—"

"I know." Penny opened the door for her and locked it once they were both out on the sidewalk. "A little like building up to this amazing future and then being left alone at the airport. Right?"

Well, fuck.

"Good night, Frankie." Penny turned and walked away, and she let herself enjoy every second of that view.

She didn't move until Penny turned a corner out of sight, then pulled out her phone as she headed for her car to see who'd texted her.

Jesus, it was Penny.

You can buy me a drink at the tavern Thursday night.

Frankie didn't pretend to understand why, but she'd take it. She felt herself flush from head to toe, almost as hard as she had when Penny had kissed her.

CHAPTER 8

*A*spen stared at the spreadsheet and rubbed her forehead. This monthly accounting session was the bane of her existence, but it had to be done. Part of running the gallery was treating it like the business it was, no matter how much she would prefer to be creating in the studio. The problem was, the business part was hard. The gallery had struggled every month since late fall to make ends meet. Last month, she hadn't taken her salary to make sure the rent was paid. This month, she wasn't going to be able to take one either, and she was working right now to figure out how she was going to get all of her artists paid what they were owed and still keep the lights on.

Summer couldn't come soon enough. The gallery needed an infusion of cash.

"Aspen?" There was a knock at her door, and she closed the spreadsheet.

"Come on in, Minnie."

"Hey, girl. Are you coming tonight?"

"I told you I would."

"What's the matter?"

"Hm?" *Dammit.* She'd never had a poker face. "Nothing, I'm fine."

"You look...not fine."

"I'm tired. I didn't sleep great last night."

"Oh. So come next week, I'm there all the time."

She could. This hadn't been the best day, she could flake on Frankie...but... "No, I'm coming. I need a distraction." Plus, she was the one that had invited Frankie after leaving her hanging. Not that she owed Frankie anything, but she wasn't a bitch.

Not completely, anyway.

Minnie had an adorably quirky smile. "Yeah? Okay, good. It starts at seven."

"Perfect. I'll see you there."

Minnie gave her a wave and closed her office door.

She'd like to say that Frankie was the furthest thing from her mind, but she couldn't lie to herself. She'd stocked her office bathroom with makeup, a toothbrush, and a tiny bottle of her favorite perfume. She'd made sure her underwear and bra matched when she got dressed this morning. She'd forgiven Patrick instantly when he asked if they could reschedule their celebratory drink. Poor Patrick. He'd fallen over himself to apologize and had been so confused when she'd shrugged and said it was fine.

She opened the spreadsheet again, intending to move some more numbers around and finish the budget for June, but after a few minutes she realized she just couldn't keep her mind on it. One more month of shortfalls and she was going to have to close the gallery and give up the studio space they occupied at the back of the building too. The rent was just too much, and she didn't have a lot of options. She could raise the rates the members paid to use the studio, and she could give up her job for good, break her responsibilities up into bits, and dole them out to the co-op members as volunteer work.

Then she'd have to find a job. She had some inherited money and no mortgage, but that money was her retirement plan as far as she was concerned, and she had to live on something. She'd already dipped into it enough.

June had to be better. That was all. It had to be damn good. And July had to be stellar. If they got that, she could get them through the summer at least and not have to close until the fall.

She sighed and closed her laptop. She was getting hangry now, and she needed a drink.

She freshened up, telling herself it wasn't for Frankie, though with her brother not coming there was really no other excuse, then made her way to Whitewater Tavern to get something to eat before Frankie showed up.

She walked in and headed straight for the bar. She wasn't here enough to know the bartenders, but she recognized a couple of people. She took a seat away from everyone and ordered a glass of Malbec, and she hadn't taken two sips when Jimmy Rainier took the seat next to her.

"Here for the karaoke?"

"Hello Aspen, it's nice to see you. Nice to see you too, Jimmy, how are you? Oh, fine. And you? Tired, Jimmy. Very tired."

"Wow. You just had a whole conversation with me and I didn't have to do jack. Cool."

"Jimmy—"

"I know, I get it. Get lost, Jimmy. I was just trying to be friendly."

She sighed. "I'm sorry. I'm hungry and I had a bad day. I'm not great company." She turned toward him. "It's not karaoke, it's open mic night, but yes, that's why I'm here. Minnie is singing."

"Oh, Minnie. She's cute."

"She's married."

"You can't be married and cute?"

"Not if you have a husband that looks like that." She flicked her eyes down to the end of the bar where Minnie was sitting with a very handsome giant.

Jimmy whistled. "Point taken."

She glanced at Jimmy again and laughed. "How's your mom?"

"Better. Painting again. You might hear from her."

"Tell her I would like that. I'm happy to come out and pick things up, if she has anything she wants to sell."

Jimmy nodded. "Thank you. I don't think she's quite there yet, the stroke has made her hand not so steady, but you know Mom. She says she's learning to work with it."

"Give her my best, okay?"

"I will do that." Jimmy's beer arrived and he picked it up off the bar. "You be good."

"Always."

Jimmy had never given up hitting on her. It was as though he thought maybe she'd just wake up one morning and decide she liked dick after all. Though if she did, it wouldn't be Jimmy she'd go after. It would be someone like Minnie's husband, Luke. She loved the name Luke. So sexy.

"Hey. You're early." Frankie took the seat that Jimmy had just left.

Shit. She really wanted to eat. "I am. You are too."

Frankie nodded and ordered a beer. "I'm starving. I thought I'd get here early and get something to eat before our *date*." Frankie put a weird emphasis on the word "date," as if she knew Aspen was going to protest.

And protest she did. "It's—"

"Not a date. I knew you were going to say that. So, okay. What is it?"

"It's…truth be told, it's a booty call. With a side of I promised someone I'd come listen to her sing."

"Okay. I'll take it. I'm having a cheeseburger first, though." Frankie grinned at her. Fuck, she was still so adorable. "Can we get a booth? Or is that too date-like? I can just go eat and come back and pretend I wasn't even here yet if you'd rather drink alone."

Same sarcastic streak too. But she was hungry, and now that she'd set their evening off with the right amount of expectation, the pressure was off to play it cool. "Let's get a booth. I want their Caesar salad, and I hate eating at the bar."

"Right on." Frankie slid off her stool and picked up both of their glasses.

"That's a date thing, Frankie."

Frankie looked at the glasses. "No, it's not. It's a…helpful thing."

She rolled her eyes and picked out a booth with a good view of the stage where Minnie would be singing. A server was there in a heartbeat with menus, and Frankie set her wine down in front of her.

"Wow, look at all these burgers." Frankie disappeared behind the tall menu.

"It's kind of what they're known for."

"California burger…cheddar cheese, iceberg lettuce, bacon, and avocado. Yes, please." Frankie closed her menu.

"You didn't pick the fries."

"I can pick fries?" Frankie opened her menu again and Aspen chuckled.

"Curly, steak, shoestring, cheesy, sweet potato, waffle, cottage…"

"Holy crap." Frankie closed the menu. "Sweet potato."

"Good choice." She planned to steal a few.

When the server returned, she ordered her chicken

Caesar, and Frankie ordered her burger and fries with glee. Rare, as always.

"I'm jealous you can eat like that."

"I'm here to ride my bike all day long five days a week and then at least once on the weekend just for fun. I think I can handle the calories."

"Oh, I didn't mean the calories. My stomach can't take rare beef, even though it's tasty."

"Oh, that. I don't know. So far so good here." Frankie leaned back in her seat and sipped her beer. "So…is this the kind of booty call where both parties get off?" Frankie's eyebrow lifted. "I just want to make sure I don't have any unrealistic expectations."

Aspen grinned smugly. "I think yes. This time."

"Oh. Good. Do we need to shake on it or something?"

"You deserved that."

"I don't know, Penny. I'm not sure anyone deserves *that*. That was—"

"Are you going to set me up for another analogy as to how you left me at the airport? Because I'd advise against giving me that opening." She softened her grin and winked at Frankie. She was done with being evil, but Frankie still had work to do.

Frankie puffed out a breath. "Right. Got it, Penny. I don't think there's room for another dagger in my heart right now."

She laughed. "It's Aspen. Do you think you could maybe try?"

"You know, whose parents name their daughter Aspen when they live in Colorado?"

"Mine." She leveled Frankie with a dead serious look.

"Okay, then. I can try." Frankie shook her head. "I don't know, though. I used to sleep with Penny. Calling out Aspen when I come instead…it kind of feels like I'd be fucking someone else." Frankie's eyes flashed heat and she shivered, the words making her nipples go hard. Thank goodness for her very structured bra. She cleared her throat.

"Okay, Frances Eleanor Hoffman."

"Oh, Jesus Christ." Frankie rolled her eyes.

"Who names their daughter Eleanor?"

"Eleanor Roosevelt was ahead of her time." Frankie stuck out her tongue.

"Aspen is a tree."

"Fine."

"Fine."

The server was back with a bowl of soft pretzels bites and a container of mustard that was spicy enough to make her nostrils sting.

Frankie waited for the server to leave; then she leaned across the table. "So…I can't scream 'Penny' when I come?"

"Aspen in public, or you won't. Again."

She absolutely loved the worried look on Frankie's face, and she laughed as Frankie replied, "Got it."

"Mm. Thank you."

"Hopefully, I'll be thanking you."

Frankie reached for a pretzel, dipped it in the mustard, and popped the whole thing into her mouth. Her eyes went wide as she chewed. "Holy fuck," she managed to say with her mouth full.

"Oh. Yeah, the mustard here is super spicy." She picked up a pretzel nugget and dipped it just a tiny bit before she ate it.

"Good to know." Frankie picked up her beer and took a long swig. "Jesus. You're going to punish me every chance you get, aren't you?"

Frankie was grinning, so she knew they were teasing and it was okay to play. "Maybe. Although I probably would have let that happen even if you hadn't—"

"Don't say it."

"That's no fun."

Frankie snorted and picked up another pretzel, this time dipping it sparingly. "I'm going to change the subject since picking on me is getting old. Let's go for mundane. How was work today?"

"That is not mundane." Not at all. She was ready for a second glass of wine already and she waved at the server.

"Oh, shit. Bad day?"

"Not a good one." She wasn't sure she wanted to share details with Frankie.

"Sorry. But Pen-*Aspen*, you actually have your gallery. I know that's what you wanted. Did you open it as soon as you moved back?"

"I made a connection before we—before I moved, and so, yes. As soon as I got back here, I hooked up with a friend who was part of this really neat, growing artist co-op, and they hired me to open Pure and run it for them. They were just about to open a common studio space so they could share the big equipment like the kiln, and it had a storefront they were originally planning to rent out. So now I keep their books, pay them when their work sells, and try to..." She shrugged. "Try to keep it going. It's not easy."

"I bet not."

Frankie was right, the gallery was her dream. It's what she wanted to do when she left UVM's business school more than anything, and she had it now. Summit Springs boasted so many amazing local artists and she got to help them reach buyers, along with some of her own work too. She was proud of what she'd accomplished so far.

Well, she'd been proud. Right now she was very worried, and more than a little embarrassed.

"It was a rough spring. And the resort isn't helping."

"What's wrong with the resort? Doesn't it bring people in?"

"It used to, but last summer they opened up all these new activities—zip lines, an ultimate frisbee course, a movie theater. They renovated their outdoor pool and opened an indoor one. They have a new restaurant too. And in the winter they added a snow-tubing hill and offered all these all-inclusive packages. People don't need to leave the resort anymore, you know?"

"So they're not coming to town." Frankie shook her head. "Damn."

"It's cold and snowy, and up there it's warm and their kids can go off on their own. Why would you leave?"

"That sucks. I wonder if that caused any issues for M and M?"

"I don't think so; there's no direct competition there. If anything, Marmot and Moose might benefit from the people that don't want that kind of experience. Or want to spend less money. The all-inclusive-resort thing is expensive."

Frankie's job was secure for sure. Marmot and Moose owned its own property and offered all kinds of year-round activities for all ages, which they expanded on a regular basis. Particularly in the summertime. They were the biggest rafting outfit in town, maybe the only one these days. And adding biking was a great idea. Frankie would do well up there.

"I know we're booked solid on Saturday, which is my first real day. Weird, because I have Monday and Tuesday off."

"That's how most places do it here. Catering to tourists who are here for long weekends."

Frankie tapped her glass as the server brought Aspen her wine and ordered another. "That's what I'm told."

"Are you nervous?"

Frankie made a face at her. "What? No. Yes. A little. Some. Shut up."

They both laughed. "I'd worry if you weren't. It'll be fine, though, this is so your thing."

"Riding is my thing. Teaching, leading, whatever...we'll see. Responsibility was never my strong suit."

"Liz and Lupe know what they're doing. They wouldn't have hired you if they thought for a second you couldn't handle it. Are you by yourself?"

"I have a team. Two other riders. They take turns with me and on the other days, they lead quieter rides on the flat trails around the lake, stuff like that."

"Wow, that's cool."

Frankie nodded. "I think so. I hope so. I'm always afraid I'll screw up."

That was Frankie's thing. Tons of "I got this" in public and just as much "What the fuck am I doing?" in private. Aspen understood that better now that she was on the what-the-fuck end of things.

She swirled her wine and made a confession. "I didn't take a salary last month, and I can't take one this month."

"Whoa. What? It's that bad?"

"The rent is tough. The work is selling, but not often enough to make the percentage I take for the co-op to be everything we need to keep the lights on."

"What are you going to do? What do the co-op folks say?"

She glanced up and met Frankie's eyes. "I haven't told them yet."

"Oh. Shit."

"I haven't told anyone but you." She didn't know why she was confiding in Frankie now either. Maybe because Frankie was an outsider. New. Frankie didn't know these people. Or maybe because Frankie had always been a good ear.

Frankie nodded slowly. "I get it. But you're going to figure it out. I know you will."

She wasn't as optimistic. "I was hoping just to wait it out, get through last month and things would turn around. Now I'm—well, if June doesn't pay off, we're done."

"I'm sorry. That sucks." Frankie touched her hand, just lightly, but enough that it made her feel less alone. "June will be better."

She picked up her wine and took another sip. "June will be better," she repeated, trying to make herself believe it. It had to be. She'd landed the sales contract with the resort's gift shop, right? That was huge. It would get some of their work up to where the people actually were. And it was summer, which brought lots of people into town whether it was for M&M or just to escape the heat farther south. That didn't change the fact that she was going to have to talk with everyone, though.

Their food arrived and Frankie grinned like a kid as her cheeseburger landed on the table. "That's what I'm talking about. Thank you." Frankie had always looked like a kid. They were the same age, but Frankie had this permanently twenty-year-old thing about her. Always moving, always trying something new and putting herself out there. Making mistakes and just shrugging them off. So fearless.

"Can I steal a fry?"

"Oh my God, please. Steal many. This is a ton of food."

She reached over and picked one up, loving the sweet potato mixed with the salt-and-pepper seasoning they put on it. "Mm. Good."

"You said we're here to listen to someone sing?"

"One of my artists. Minnie. She's over there at the bar."

"Oh, damn. She's hot. I guess the guy next to her is her boyfriend?"

"Husband."

"Damn. They're both pretty."

"Right?" She chuckled. Frankie wasn't a label type but if she were, Aspen would put her in the pansexual category. It used to make her crazy, feeling like every person they walked by was potential competition. At least that's how her college brain had worked at the time: No one was safe. And it didn't help that she'd been the jealous type back then.

Maybe still, she wasn't sure.

"Is she good?"

"Honestly, I don't know. I've never come out for an open mic night before."

"Never? Really?"

"To be fair, I didn't even know she sang here regularly until recently. So it's not like I've been avoiding it or anything."

"Are you still a hermit?"

"Shut up." She rolled her eyes at her college nickname. She'd earned it for heading for a throwing wheel on Friday nights when everyone else was going out to parties. But she'd loved those nights; it was always quiet in the pottery studio.

"Okay, introvert then."

"I suppose. I'm not avoiding anyone, though. I see people all day: people in the gallery, people in the studio, I have friends, my brother…I'm not hiding or anything."

Frankie tilted her head but didn't say whatever she was thinking.

"What?"

"Nothing."

"Spit it out, Frankie."

"If you have friends, why am I the first person you're telling about the gallery?"

She pursed her lips and shook her head. "Shut up."

Frankie chuckled and picked up her burger. "Okay."

Frankie took a few big bites of her burger, the kind you couldn't talk around, so the table went quiet for a few minutes apart from "Mmm" and "How's your salad?" She already regretted telling Frankie about the gallery—and also not. It was out now; that meant it was real and she actually did have to deal with it.

"Hello, gentlefolk of Summit Springs!"

They glanced up from their meal when a tall blond woman started the evening off on stage with the microphone.

"Welcome to open mic night. I see a few regulars out there, so I can tell you it's going to be a good one. A few new faces too. Don't be shy if you're new, we all were once. Get your name on the list at the bar and step on up. We're looking forward to hearing you. A few rules: One, everyone gets applause. If you're here, if you're sitting over at this end of the place, you're here to listen, so show everyone some appreciation. Two, no tipping or throwing money, under-wear, or food at the stage or otherwise acting like animals, because I will personally bounce you out. Three, do tip your servers and have fun. First up..."

"Is she the owner?" Frankie asked, picking up her beer.

"No, she works here. I can't remember her name, but I have seen her carry people out by their belt, so I'd keep your undies on." She winked at Frankie, who laughed happily, eyes lighting up.

"Got it."

The first act wasn't singing, it was stand-up, and the guy was hilarious. Some celebrity jokes, some political ones, and even some only the locals would understand, which got the most reaction of all. She drank her wine and listened to Frankie's easy laugh, remembering how much she liked it. Part of her was close to forgiving Frankie, at least enough to give her another chance. But a more stubborn part of her was still defensive and not about to get her heart broken again. Not just broken, stomped on. Humiliated. God, she'd felt like a complete idiot. How could she have been so wrong about where things stood? About who Frankie was?

And who was Frankie now?

She wanted that touch, though. Frankie remembered just how to get her off, like it had mattered to her. And maybe it had. And her ex had come a very long way and uprooted herself to be here, to find her.

What did it really mean?

"If I could sing like that, I'd be on my way to Vegas. Or LA or New York or something. He's amazing."

She blinked herself back to the table. Dan Killington was singing, he was a crooner that sang at every wedding she'd been to in town, and also had a regular gig up at the resort. He was good. She wasn't sure why he stayed in town either, but he was a nice guy.

"He is good, right? Dan's friendly too, and local. I went to high school with him. He's the kind of guy that pays for coffee for the person behind him in line on a rainy Monday morning just because, you know?"

"That's cool."

"Right?" They applauded for Dan as he finished and Dan waved before putting the mic down and leaving the stage.

"Next up we have Minnie Jackson." The MC said from the side of the stage. It was bugging her that she couldn't remember the woman's name. "Originally from Los Angeles, Minnie came to Summit Springs for an artists' retreat and never left. We're glad she stayed. You should check out her work just up the street at Pure Art Gallery. Welcome, Minnie."

There was loud applause and Minnie smiled as she picked up the mic. "Thanks, y'all." She obviously had some fans in the audience.

Minnie got their attention instantly; Frankie even turned away from her fries to listen. Some people were just born talented. Her voice was smooth like honey and rich, and the bluesy song she'd picked was perfect for her. The whole place went still as Minnie sang—servers stopped walking; even folks at the bar turned their heads as Minnie's sexy voice filled the place.

Aspen's attention was divided, though, between Minnie's song and Frankie's face. This was the reason she'd missed something. Everything Frankie did was honest. Her appreciation for Minnie's performance was all over her face. Frankie was a terrible liar, she was bad at secrets, she said what was on her mind. It still baffled her that Frankie hadn't shown up at the airport that morning.

She'd never had one second of doubt in her mind.

It didn't make sense then, and it wasn't any clearer now.

Minnie's song ended and the place went nuts with cheers and applause. Minnie laughed and waved and thanked everyone a couple of times.

"Jesus, Penny. She's amazing."

She nodded, watching Minnie leave the stage. "I had no idea. I need to—will you excuse me for a minute?" She hopped up and intercepted Minnie on her way back to her husband at the bar.

"Hey, girl. You made it."

"Minnie, that was amazing."

"Thank you. It's fun. I saw you sitting over there with your date. Is that the mad sex ex?"

She blushed. "Yes. That's Frankie."

Minnie nodded. "She's hot. How's it going?"

"It's…going. Listen, can we have lunch tomorrow?"

"Oh, for sure. Everything okay?" Minnie's concern was so sweet and so genuine.

"I just need to run something by you."

"Sure. Sounds good. Meet here around noon?"

"Why not? Thanks, Minnie. You were amazing, I'm not missing this next week."

Minnie gave her a quick hug. "Thank you for coming. Sounds odd maybe, but it means a lot."

"I'm so blown away. Thank you for the invitation. I'll see you tomorrow." She let Minnie walk away, then went back to Frankie.

"Sorry, I just had to—"

"Yep." Frankie nodded, interrupting her thought.

"What are you grinning at?"

"It's just—I'm happy to be here, and that you let me in a little. And you're still so fucking beautiful, Penny."

She blushed again, the warmth spreading up into her face so fast there was no hiding it.

Frankie stood before she could sit. "I paid the bill."

"Oh." Aspen swallowed. "Thank you." She followed Frankie to the door, and Frankie held it for her.

"So…my place is kind of awkward…"

"My brother and Heather are out with friends." Like she had a choice anyway. A bunkhouse was no place for what they were about to get up to.

"Oh, good. I mean, your office was nice, but—"

She laughed. "Beggars can't be choosers, you know."

"Oh, I know. And I was begging. I'm still begging."

"I bet you are."

Frankie took her hand and she let it happen, and every few steps Frankie would look over at her.

"What?" she finally asked. "Just say it."

"Nothing to say, I just like watching you."

The blushing thing was embarrassing, but it made Frankie smile.

"Am I driving with you?"

"I have to be back down here early for work, you?"

Frankie shook her head, blond hair blowing in the evening breeze. "No. I'm on my own time until Saturday."

"I'll drive. What if it snows? No point in digging out two cars."

"It's June."

"Oh. Right." Okay, small talk was a bad idea, she was losing brain cells to her hormones.

They wandered through the parking garage to the second level. It wasn't like Aspen could forget where she parked—she had a reserved spot—but she was distracted and when she spotted the green Subaru she headed for it. "You still drive this thing, huh?"

"You'd never know it was coming up on a hundred and fifty. It made the trip from Vermont like it was made for the highway." Frankie had always loved her car.

"Oh. My truck is...uh." She glanced around. "Over there."

Frankie chuckled. "You drive a truck?"

"It was my mom's. It's in great shape." Patrick drove it for a bit after Mom died, and then he took Dad's bigger truck after they lost Dad last year. "It's handy for moving things—art, supplies for the studio, you know. Stuff."

Frankie got into the passenger side easily. She wasn't tall but she was fit, and she hauled herself up like it was nothing. They left the garage, and Frankie turned on the radio. She'd never regretted living twenty minutes from town until just this moment, when wanting someone had to wait, and not only that but she had to concentrate on the winding climb up to the house.

Aspen liked how quiet but restless Frankie was beside her. Every so often she'd sing along with the chorus of what-ever was on the radio, but mostly Frankie was trying hard to be patient and it showed. Shifting in her seat, looking at her, looking out the window.

"I like your hair down," she finally said, breaking the silence. "And blond."

"Yeah?" Frankie ran her fingers through it. "Blond is natural."

"I know. But it was pink and black when I saw it last."

"It was. That phase ended when I suddenly had bills to pay. Hair dye is expensive."

"Is it?" Aspen had never dyed her hair. Ever. It was dark and it would have taken more effort than she ever wanted to deal with.

"Yeah. And I like things like food and heat." Frankie's warm hand slid across her leg and she inhaled, calling on some patience of her own. She imagined reaching over, slipping her hand between Frankie's strong thighs. How she'd ever fallen in with an athlete she'd never know, but she was looking forward to touching Frankie again.

"Heat is good." She'd taken her parents' master suite at the house. There was a fireplace and a sitting area in the bedroom. Warm was good. The view was better. "Almost there." She took the last big corner carefully. It was night now and although she was used to driving this route, she had a healthy respect for the road.

"Thank God." Frankie chuckled and she joined in.

"It'll be worth the wait." She knew that. They both did. Even if it really was just a booty call.

It was just a booty call. Yes. For sure.

A booty call…and a sleepover.

When they pulled in, the only lights on were the lamps at the driveway entrance and the two up by the house.

"I could have used those lights to guide me when I came up here for dinner."

"It wasn't dark yet, was it?"

"No, but finding this driveway was still tricky."

"Dad put the lights in when Patrick learned how to drive. He kept missing the driveway, and your options are reverse, or turn around a mile farther up."

"A mile?"

"Yep. Not fun in bad weather."

"I bet not." Frankie pulled her close as they climbed the steps to the porch and the front door. "Oh, man. The moon."

Aspen looked out at the mountains. The full moon was so bright some of the peaks cast shadows. So amazing. "It's the prettiest place on earth. We're on top of the world up here."

"We are." Frankie startled her with a hungry kiss, and she surprised herself by welcoming it warmly, circling her arms around Frankie's shoulders. They explored each other, tongues tangling and gliding together. Frankie's fingers roamed over her back, and she drew hers through Frankie's soft hair.

"You let it get long."

"Not really on purpose, I'm just lazy. Do you like it?" Frankie's eyes shone in the moonlight, light enough to still look blue.

"I do, actually. And you don't seem like the lazy type."

Frankie leaned closer and kissed her just under her ear, then whispered. "I'm not lazy about you. I'm ready to give you everything I've got."

She broke out in goose bumps, and her nipples grew tight and hard. The moonlight was romantic and beautiful, but they could see it from bed after she got her orgasms. "Come on."

Frankie laughed softly at being dragged to the front door. "Hungry, baby?"

"I just want your lazy ass to be naked." She grinned back, opened the door, and locked it behind them. "Down that way."

"You don't want another glass of wine, first?"

"Nope."

"Dessert? I know you have ice cream." Frankie teased, as

Aspen herded her along the hallway. "You always have ice cream."

"Shut up." She couldn't help but chuckle. Frankie was adorable when she was playing.

"Whoa, look at this room." Frankie walked right into the master bedroom, and flopped into one of the overstuffed chairs by the fireplace. "Look at your view!"

She stayed by the bed and started undressing slowly. "The view is better over here."

"Oh. Yes, it is." Frankie stood again and came to her quickly. "Much better. I've been waiting for this view all night."

They both undressed. She hung her clothing neatly over a chair and, predictably, Frankie's dropped in a heap on the floor. The familiar scenario was comforting and put her even more at ease. This side of Frankie obviously hadn't changed much, and Aspen was happy about that. This was the side she wanted right now.

She drew the covers down and Frankie stretched her out on the bed. Frankie explored her skin with curious fingers, touching her everywhere as if making sure she was real. It made her toes curl and all her intimate muscles clench with need. "What are you doing?"

Frankie gave her a hot look as she bent to a begging nipple. "Turning you on."

"Oh." Fuck yes, she was.

She sighed at the first touch of Frankie's tongue, arching toward it. Frankie bathed that nipple until Aspen moaned, then turned her attention to the other. Aspen tucked her hand under Frankie's hair and caught her nape, arched harder and let her body ask for more, but no matter how much she begged, Frankie still took it slowly. By the time Frankie's fingers pushed into her curls, her breath was coming in soft pants and she was wet with wanting.

"Yes," she whispered and caught one of Frankie's sweet breasts in her hand.

Frankie pushed into the touch, moving high enough that Aspen was able to suck a nipple into her mouth as Frankie's fingers slid gently over her clit.

"Yes," she said again, but it wasn't enough, and she rolled her hips into Frankie's hand.

"You feel so good, Penny." The tightness in Frankie's voice was the first sign of Frankie's arousal and Aspen took advantage, raising a knee between Frankie's thighs.

Frankie's fingers slid inside her and they rocked together, bodies rising higher, making them both breathless. Aspen pushed a hand between them to replace her thigh and found Frankie every bit as ready as she was. Frankie gasped and that was the end of the gentle build. They moaned and thrust and rolled, finding that sweet spot where they were both hungry and striving.

She'd been so focused on Frankie's honest need that her own orgasm surprised her. She was suddenly just on the edge and the next time Frankie's palm ground over her clit, she was done. She gasped loudly, moaning again and again, until Frankie's cry cut through the fog.

"Yes, baby!" Aspen watched Frankie's face go from strained to stunned to total nirvana, all of it so beautiful. Familiar in her memory too, yet somehow still new to her all over again.

They kissed and tried to breathe while Frankie hung over her and the aftershocks moved through them both. Then Frankie flopped to one side of her heavily. "Oh, fuck."

"Mmm. Yes, it was." They both chuckled. "I let you come this time."

Frankie snorted. "As if I'd have allowed anything else. It was a long drive up here."

She sighed and rolled toward Frankie, determined to

enjoy the afterglow and keep the reasons this was a bad idea away for now. She deserved more. Answers. An explanation. But she'd been honest about what this was—she'd wanted Frankie in her bed. She'd needed to be touched. It wasn't a crime. And it wasn't a contract.

It definitely made things complicated, though.

She rested her head on Frankie's shoulder, and a strong arm curled around her back. This part wasn't complicated at least. This her body understood.

CHAPTER 9

*P*enny was already up and showered when Frankie opened her eyes. Frankie could see her through the open bathroom door, doing her makeup in the mirror, her hair up in a towel. She watched quietly, admiring the line of Penny's body as she bent over the sink, leaning closer to the mirror to put on mascara. Penny was barefoot and so beautiful, her lovely breasts and perfect ass in a matching blue lingerie set. Or purple. Lavender? Periwinkle. Something blueish-purple and hot.

This would have been the perfect morning to wake up, kiss, and run. Morning-afters could be awkward, but this one…man. Last night was supposed to be a booty call, but it felt like a lot more than that to her. And now Penny was her ride into town, so she was going to have to smile and play house a little, and pretend like she was an adult.

She got up, scratching fingers through her hair as she shuffled around, looking for her clothing. Eventually she found it, folded neatly on the end of the bed instead of dumped on the floor wherever she had left it. *Thanks, Mom,* she thought, even though she should have expected it. Penny was like that, and it was always hard to tell if it was passive-aggressive, or just being helpful. Today it was probably a little of both.

She picked up her T-shirt after pulling on her underwear and bra but dropped it back onto the bed, deciding to wait. Why not give Penny something to look at? It was the only leverage she had at the moment, so she decided to use it.

"Morning," she said as she stepped through the bathroom door.

"Morning." Penny didn't so much as hesitate while brushing her hair, or even glance Frankie's way.

Mhm. Awkward. Probably should have thought this through better and brought her own car.

She wet her fingers, combed them through her hair, and reached for a black scrunchie sitting on the counter. "Can I borrow this?"

Penny looked over, then at the mirror. "Sure."

"Do you have a towel I could—"

"Help yourself. Tall cabinet next to the tub. There's a little stash of toothbrushes in the bottom too."

"Thanks." Washcloth. Towel. Hideous hot-pink tooth-brush. *Good to go.*

She washed up and brushed her teeth while Penny ran the hairdryer so talking didn't have to be a thing. She hadn't thought to bring an overnight bag—she honestly hadn't thought overnight was going to be involved. She'd assumed the tavern thing was so they could drink and have it out. Again. Penny seemed to enjoy making sure she knew what a piece of shit she was. A hot piece of shit maybe, one that Penny wanted on some level, but still the lowest of the low.

She wanted to explain. Not as an excuse for breaking Penny's heart, but so Penny would understand why hers was broken too. But she wasn't sure how, or when—maybe Penny wouldn't care. Maybe Penny didn't want more than this from her. Or maybe she wanted to start over. Who knew? Penny had always been the kind of woman you had to read carefully. Pay attention to. And she was a complicated mystery right now.

Frankie was dressed and ready before Penny and didn't really want to stand around. "I can make some coffee."

"It's a big pot. I just get it in town."

"Oh. Right, sure. You want to strip the bed?"

"I'll do that later. Thank you."

"Okay…" She rocked on her toes. *Fucking. Awkward.* "You were amazing last night. Hot. Beautiful." Oh, good. That was sure to make things less awkward. She would have rolled her eyes at herself if she didn't think Penny would catch it.

But Penny blushed, and everything was suddenly better. Real.

"Thank you. You were—"

"Shh." She hushed Penny and stepped close to her to give her a kiss on the cheek. Just a gesture. An overture. "We're talking about you."

Penny smiled and nodded. "*I*…am glad I invited you to come home with me."

That was good, right? "Yeah? Me too."

Penny pulled a pair of black flats out of her closet and stepped into them. "If we go now, there will be plenty of time for coffee."

Was that an invitation to sit for coffee, or just Penny saying, "Let's go, I need my caffeine"? She was captive for this trip, so she figured she'd find out.

"I'm ready." She followed Penny out to the truck. She needed a shower, but there wasn't much point; she was headed up the trails this morning.

"Check out the fog in the mountains." As they left the driveway, Penny pointed to some bright, fluffy, low-lying clouds that seemed to cut the mountain range in half. "You know how they talk about the fog lifting? It literally does that. The low clouds get pushed up as the day warms up and dissipate above the peaks by late morning. It's neat. I love it."

"Neat." She looked out the truck window. "My weather app said rain today."

"Oh, yeah? I didn't know that. Well, then this fog might not go away; it might get trapped under the storm clouds as they move in."

It was sunny right now, but windy too. Her ride would be an adventure anyway.

"You start work tomorrow?"

Wow. That was suddenly so real her stomach did a flip-flop. "Yeah. My first group goes up at eight. I'm kinda nervous."

"You're going to be great. This is your thing, and now you're getting paid for it. It doesn't get better than that. Trust me, I know."

She smiled at Penny. "I guess you would." The truck was quiet after that until they took the last turn into town and Penny pulled into the parking garage. Then they both started talking at the same time, which made them laugh.

Penny put the truck in park. "You go."

"Okay. Well, I'm off on Monday and I was thinking…"

"Let's touch base on Sunday. Maybe we can go hiking or something."

"I'd love that—wait. You hike?"

Penny grinned. "Not much, but it sounded better than 'Let's take a walk.' We…should probably talk."

"Oh."

"A good talk. Like a clear the air talk."

Frankie sighed. "Okay. I know I—you deserve—"

Penny put a hand on her knee. "Monday."

She nodded. "Right. Monday."

"Until then, we have afterglow."

Frankie winked at her and got out of the truck.

~

"Wow, Frankie. What happened?"

Frankie rolled her eyes and sighed at Lucy. "I'm fine. My bike skidded out from under me on the mountain this morning. It looks worse than it is."

"That last whoop-de-do was more of a whoop-de-don't, huh?" Alex chuckled, proud of their pun. They gave Lucy a knowing look, then went back to doctoring up the scrape on her knee. It was a big patch of angry skin, but that was all.

"I guess so." Lucy got a Coke out of the fridge. "Didn't you say you were going for the easy ride today?"

Frankie nodded, embarrassed. "Yep. Intermediate trail. It was nice. There are a few fun parts that aren't too technical and lots of places to pull off and rest or wait for stragglers. Some of them have great views too."

"So you ride the tough ones and come home without a scrape, but you take the easy one and—"

"Shut up."

Alex laughed and Lucy eyed Frankie. "That's what you get for not coming home last night."

"Mhm. Girl's mind was on the wrong set of curves."

She shook her head. "Stop that." *Dammit.* Alex was probably right, but she wasn't going to admit it. She'd had her mind on this thing with Penny for sure.

"So what happened?" Lucy sat on the floor and watched as Alex tortured Frankie with hydrogen peroxide.

"I don't know exactly. I'd stopped at a pull-over point halfway down the bike trail for some water and to get a lay of the land." She'd been scoping the trail out and a couple of others like it for some all-ages guided rides in the middle of next week.

It was a good day for the shorter, easier rides because she hadn't trusted the weather. Even now the sky was looking more threatening than the weather app forecast seemed to suggest. "I guess I'll watch the playback from my GoPro and see."

"You record your rides?"

"Almost always. I keep a journal with notes on every trail I ride so I know if I want to go back or not. Or if someone asks me, I can give them all the deets. I used to write them all from memory, but with the camera I can put in more details and make great notes describing the features and things to look for. I post the good ones on YouTube once I've had time to edit them."

This time she had notes to make about her equipment too. She hadn't ridden her own bike, she'd taken one of the rentals on the trail today. She'd wanted to try it so she'd be familiar with the equipment her guests would be using. It was a nice bike, had good action and stability. It had felt a little jangly to her, looser than she was used to, but that was what happened when you were picky about your own equipment. Everything else felt weird.

"Oh, yeah? I'm going to look you up. That's cool. You must have a lot of journals."

"I have three right now. But I started a new one just for Colorado." And it was probably going to be full by the end of the summer and then some.

"Are you making a guidebook?"

She blinked at Lucy. "A guidebook?" She'd never thought about that.

"Sure. Why not?"

"I'm sure there are already a hundred of them." But what a great idea for the off-season if there weren't.

"So, check it out and see," Alex agreed. "It's a great idea."

Lucy crossed her legs and leaned on one arm, watching

her. "Assuming you can focus on anything but the ex-girlfriend."

"Right?" Alex pinned her with a playful look. "Is she still an ex?"

She snorted. "Nosy."

"We're living vicariously through you. I'm only here for the summer and Alex is never single, so—"

"Wrong. I am always single. I just date a lot."

She was grateful that the conversation shifted to Alex's circular and complicated love life. She didn't know what she and Penny were now. Exes with benefits? It wasn't like Penny had officially taken her back, but she hadn't officially not either. This morning could have been super sticky but it wasn't, they'd had a nice ride into town.

Except for that embarrassing bit where she'd tried to kiss Penny good-bye and Penny had stepped away and given her a wave instead.

A wave. After being totally naked the night before. Not even a quick smooch.

Penny was so frustrating. Such a...control freak.

It was that control thing that was really making Frankie crazy. The worst part was that she felt like she had to let Penny have it right now. She was the screw-up. She was the one asking to be forgiven. She'd put all her cards out there, and Penny was kind of collecting them one by one. She was calling all the shots.

Not that Penny had kept that careful control last night. Nope. Penny was as beautiful as ever, as hungry as ever, and they'd both lost themselves for a while. Penny hadn't been embarrassed, and she hadn't been apologetic. It was...perfect.

They had the sex thing down. The rest was—

"Earth to Frankie..."

She blinked. "Sorry, what?" She looked more closely and

her knee was neatly wrapped in some light first-aid gauze. "Oh. Thanks."

"Jesus, Frankie. No wonder you wiped out. Are you okay? Did you hit your head? Let me see."

"I'm fine, it's not my head."

"I'm looking." Alex wasn't taking no for an answer, and Frankie sighed.

"It's inside my head, not outside."

Lucy nodded at her. "Now you're talking."

"The physical stuff is good. Amazing. The rest is really fucking messy, you know?"

Alex's head tilted. "Aw. You've got it bad, Frankie."

"I know. And she's—it's my fault and she's mad. She has every right to be."

"So you're groveling."

She nodded emphatically. "I am totally groveling."

"Well, you can't grovel forever. And you've got work to do, so get your head back in the game. You're going to ride that bike right off the side of the mountain."

She frowned at Alex. They were right. She did have a job to do. "Yeah, that's a legit concern."

Alex shook their head. "Listen. Whatever mistakes you made, she's already at least partly forgiven you. Whether she accepts that or not, it's true, or you would have slept in your own bed last night, right?"

That, or Penny was never going to want more than a booty call. "Maybe?"

Alex sighed. "Not maybe. For sure. And I'm sure you had what you thought was a good reason—you don't seem like the asshole type to me. So don't give it all away; you get to have feelings too."

"Okay." Had she had a good reason? Yes. And she totally had feelings. Big feelings. A giant cocktail of love and regret, and they didn't mix well.

Lucy clucked her tongue. "Frankie."

"Okay. Yes. I won't grovel forever. Just...for a while."

Alex caught her eyes and held them. "Good. We're here for you, Frankie. Vent to us, and keep it together on the mountain."

"Yeah. I got you. Work hard, play hard, leave Penny off the trails. It's a deal. Thanks."

Lucy stood up. "When are you seeing her again?"

"Uh...Monday. We're both off. She wants to talk." Finally. God, this was so overdue.

"Okay, good. You want to talk too."

She nodded slowly. "Yes. And, also no." She was dreading the conversation they needed to have. She just hoped that Penny would see how stuck she'd felt.

"Yeah, well. Hard talks are like that."

"Ice cream isn't complicated." Lucy hopped up from the floor. "So, I'm taking you for ice cream."

She smiled at Lucy. "Yeah? I am so in." She got up and checked her knee. It didn't hurt, but the skin felt a little tight. Nothing that would stop her from riding tomorrow, though.

"Right on. I'm in too. Business is picking up around here. We're going to be too tired for ice cream soon."

"You can be too tired for ice cream?"

Alex laughed. "Oh, you wait and see, honey."

Oh, boy. Well, she was ready. She was even looking forward to it. "Mint chocolate chip, here I come."

CHAPTER 10

*T*he real mistake had been letting Frankie into her bed.

Aspen didn't regret the sex itself, or dinner. That hot quickie in her office wasn't an issue either. The problem was that now her bed felt big. Empty. She hadn't slept well, and she hadn't been able to get out of it fast enough this morning.

She didn't understand, though. She'd had a few people stay the night before, even several nights. It wasn't like she'd been celibate for the last two years. It didn't make sense, but somehow, this was different. This time she specifically wanted Frankie back in it.

She missed Frankie. Again. Or still. Whatever.

Ugh.

Aspen sighed and left her office, headed for the coffeemaker in the studio. Was it really Frankie that she missed? Or was it just the habit of having Frankie around? A habit after two years apart? Was there such a thing?

"Morning, Aspen." Minnie gave her a wave. "You throwing today?"

"That's the plan." Once she got her head in the right place.

Or the wrong place. Whichever. She threw well when she was emotional too. Sometimes it helped her focus. Apathy didn't make good art.

"Coffee is still brewing."

"Damn." She looked at the coffeemaker from across the room and decided to put the kettle on for tea instead. Take that, habits. "I'm impatient. I'll get tea." The kettle was in her office, so she made her way there.

"Bye," Minnie called after her, laughing.

She didn't know what it was exactly that had made it hard to sleep—to sleep alone—last night, but she knew what it wasn't. It wasn't the part of her that had wanted to call Frankie every day for nearly two months after she'd landed in Denver. It wasn't the part of her that had looked out the airplane window or pretended to sleep all the way here from Burlington so people sitting near her wouldn't know she was crying. It definitely wasn't those parts, because those pieces still hurt sometimes. Not like the appetite-stealing, heavy sort of depression she'd finally pulled herself out of, but that first time she'd seen Frankie, when Frankie had ambushed her in her own house…?

Mhm.

It's a good thing she did all her fighting with words or all that athletic strength wouldn't have done Frankie one damn bit of good. She'd been pissed. And after Frankie left the house that night, she'd felt a lot of other hard things and she'd cried herself to sleep. Again.

It was awful to want something so badly and be so afraid of it at the same time. Or someone. Frankie could break her heart all over again if Aspen let her, and it was starting to feel like she was going to give Frankie that chance.

But first, she needed to understand why this was the situation they were in at all.

Because there was no "why." There was no reason she had

ever managed to find or even guess for why Frankie would just no-show at the airport. No forgivable one, anyway. Over time, she'd decided that Frankie had just been lying to her. That Frankie was just too self-involved to care about anyone else. Something about Frankie was a lie. It was easier to get over her once she'd decided that because at least Aspen had a reason to work with and something to be angry about.

But now—if it was actually all a lie, what was Frankie doing here? She didn't need Summit Springs on her résumé if she wanted to be a mountain bike guide, she could have gone anywhere. She chose this place, her place, on purpose. Whether she'd said it or not—and she'd better say it soon— Frankie had followed her here. Frankie was here for her.

So, was it a lie or not?

And if it wasn't—

Aspen put the electric kettle on and picked out her favorite tangerine tea, annoyed with herself. She had work to do, and going down this road only brought her back to two years ago before she'd made any progress in getting over someone she'd once thought of as her soul mate.

There was a knock at her door, and it startled her, but she was grateful for it. She needed to get out of this headspace. "Come in."

Richie poked his head in from the gallery where he was working today. "Hey, Boss."

"How's business?" She asked the question out of habit, then realized she didn't really want to know the answer.

"Quiet. And Bucky is here."

"Bucky?" *Fuck*. Her confusion over Frankie and all of that baggage was far preferable to a conversation with him right now.

"Landlord Bucky?" Richie said, crossing his eyes, teasing.

"I know who Bucky is, dork." She faked a laugh and went to her desk. "Send him in." She knew why he was here, or she assumed she did, and her stomach did somersaults waiting for him to come through the door.

"Good morning, Ms. Young." Bucky Christian was a good landlord and a sweet guy, but something about the way he called her "Ms. Young" didn't bode well for her. He tipped his expensive cowboy hat and gave her a smile that was already apologetic and he hadn't said anything to apologize for yet.

"Hey, Bucky. Have a seat."

"Uh-huh. Thank you." He sat.

They stared at each other for a second; then both of them spoke at once.

"Sorry." She chuckled, embarrassed.

Bucky nodded. "I guess you know why I'm here. How about I go first, shall I?"

She sighed and tapped the side of her empty tea mug. "Sure. Go ahead."

Bucky leaned back in his chair, watching her. "Your rent is late."

"I know. We're still in the grace period, though, right?"

"Mmhm." Bucky nodded slowly and looked her right in the eyes. "You are. But, in my experience, folks who invoke the grace period instead of pulling out their checkbooks when I remind them their rent is late are in enough trouble that they're gonna overshoot the grace anyway."

She bit her lip and nodded back. "Yeah. But I'm working on it."

"So, here's what I do."

Oh, fuck. She really thought she could negotiate something. "Listen, Bucky, maybe we can—"

"Aspen, you'd do well just to listen to me."

"Sorry." She bit her lips together and nodded. *Fuck fuck fuck.*

"This happens in a tourist town, especially with newer

businesses that haven't figured out yet how much cash to put away in the good months to cover the bad ones."

Bucky had hit the nail on the head there, hadn't he? "I just didn't realize how bad—"

Bucky put a hand up to stop her, but his smile was indulgent. "Will you please stop interrupting me?"

She sighed. "Yes." *Jesus.* This was such a mess. "I'm sorry, Bucky."

"You're anxious. I understand. So, what I will do is, I will meet you halfway this month. I'll forgive half the rent, and the other half will get spread out over the rest of the year to get you caught up."

Oh. That meant no rent payment this month at all? She dared to breathe a little. "Oh, my God. Bucky, that's so nice of you." Maybe they weren't going to have to close shop. Maybe she could do this.

"Nice, good business…" Bucky cocked his head one way, then the other, and chuckled. "Six of one, half a dozen of the other."

"Well, I'm going with nice. And generous."

"Next month, though, we're going to have to talk hard if you don't have the rent."

"Okay. Yes. I hear you." She'd have it. Somehow.

"Aspen. Come to me *before* it's late. You understand me? Before. Not after. Don't lie to yourself, because then it just gets more complicated, and I get impatient. I'm not interested in evicting people, but I also need to pay my bills. So, we talk if it comes to that, okay?"

She took a deep breath and swallowed back all the crazy emotions she was suddenly dealing with. "Yes. I understand."

"*Before.*"

"Before. I promise." She hoped it didn't come to that.

Bucky nodded and stood. "Your dad would be proud of you, Aspen."

Oh, God. Now she really was going to cry. "Thanks, Bucky. I appreciate this so much."

"Good luck with everything. We'll talk again soon."

Bucky offered her a hand and she shook it. She kind of wanted a hug, but he was her landlord now, not the guy her dad used to go fishing and hunting with. "Yes. Thank you."

"Have a good day." Bucky let himself out and she waited until he'd closed the door, then collapsed in her chair and let a few tears out.

CHAPTER 11

$\mathcal{F}$rankie watched the EMTs as they got Peter into a collar and stabilized his obviously broken arm, wondering if her first day at work was also going to be her last. What the hell had happened? One minute everything was fine, and the next—well, biking was like that, accidents happened suddenly and randomly, but calling the EMTs on her very first day?

They were efficient and no-nonsense as they worked, and she was really impressed. Peter was awake and talking, even laughing a little with them, so Frankie was pretty sure the guy was going to be okay, but this was a bummer of a way to end his vacation.

And she still had a few of his friends to get down the rest of the mountain.

Her morning tour had gone like a dream. She'd had good riders that were able to articulate their skills and their limits, and they'd had a blast. The afternoon one was just the opposite so far—these kids were daredevils, but she had a job to do, and come hell or high water she was going to get the rest of this crew to the parking lot in one piece.

"Hey, guys?" One of the EMTs waved to Peter's friends. "Grab his bike, and we'll load it up."

To their credit, they got right to it.

"It's Frankie, right?"

"Yeah." Frankie walked over to the ATV they'd brought up from the base. Peter was sitting in it, broken arm wrapped in what was essentially bright-orange bubble wrap. It was immobilized and strapped to his chest.

"We're going to take him down now, and we have to move pretty slow. So stay here for at least twenty minutes and let us get out of your way; then you can open the trail again and continue on."

"Thanks." She nodded. "Got it."

"You're new up here, right?"

She puffed out a breath. "Yeah. Great showing for my first day, huh?"

"Actually, I was going to say you did well. You did everything right while you waited for us—you even left his helmet on, which a lot of folks ignore. You're not new to biking, for sure."

Well, that made her feel a bit better. "Thanks." She wasn't new to injuries either; she'd had a few herself.

"I'm Evie, this is Steve. Here's my card. If we're gone when you get to the parking lot, give me a call and I'll catch you up and tell you where his friends can find him. We can't take anyone else with us, there isn't room."

"Yeah, I get that. I'll call. Thanks very much."

Evie climbed onto a little jump seat in the back of the ATV, secured their supplies, and they were off.

She turned around and looked at Peter's buddies. They all had names, but she'd completely forgotten them with all the stress. God, they were young, though. She was only twenty-five, but even so, these kids seemed like babies to her.

"They're taking Peter to the hospital. We'll get all the details when we get down the mountain."

They nodded like a bunch of bobblehead dolls.

"We have to keep the trail closed for a bit so the ATV can get out of the way, so grab some water and a snack. This will be our last stop."

They sat for a while and she asked them questions just to pass the time and keep the mood light. Where were they from, what colleges did they go to, where was their favorite ride? Anything she could think of until it was safe to open the trail again.

"He wasn't riding crazy," one of the guys said, shaking his head. "I mean, he was jibbin' it some, but not crazy shit."

She'd been in the lead and Peter had been right behind her, so she'd have to take the kid's word for it. "Okay. Well, accidents happen. People wipe out. I certainly have. The important thing is to keep your head on the trail on the way down." She kept her tone serious, but a little voice in the back of her head was riding her about her own wipeout the day before and where her head had been.

They all nodded slowly.

"Listen, folks. There's nothing you can do for Peter right now, right? He's in good hands, and you have to get off this mountain one way or another. Get your head in the game, and enjoy it. It's okay." She wasn't going to get too aggressive, but this trail required some confidence. "You'll be there for Peter as soon as you can be."

That seemed to click with them, and they all went for their bikes.

"I'm going to hike up and open the trail. You stay clear until I get back in case riders come through."

The rest of the ride was slower but still fun. After a few minutes everyone loosened up, and she even heard some whoops behind her. That was good. She still felt responsible, and she had this awful feeling she was going to catch hell for this, but she followed her own advice, kept her focus, and everyone else made it to the parking lot safely, mostly with smiles on their faces.

Evie wasn't kidding about how slowly the ATV had to move, because she was just closing the ambulance doors as they all came off the trail and rode into the parking lot.

"Evie? Can someone go with?"

"Yeah, if they come right now."

"I got it." One of the kids handed his bike and his helmet off and jogged across the lot.

"We're headed to Summit Gen. Helmet is trash, sorry. But his bike is over there." Evie pointed to the bike against a railing and let the kid into the back of the ambulance with Peter.

"Got it. Thank you so much."

Evie gave her a wave, and they all watched the ambulance drive off. The EMTs must have been pretty confident Peter was okay, because they didn't speed off or turn the sirens on, just the lights.

"Okay." She turned to the kids. "You all good?"

"Totally. Thank you so much."

She started shaking hands. "You're welcome. I'm sorry about—"

"Nah, it's cool, bro. Shit happens. I broke my collarbone last summer. This joker here has sprained pretty much everything. You were great. Thank you so much."

She let herself breathe. "Those last couple of turns are awesome, right?"

"You know it. I bet we come again. We have a few days left here. Thanks for all the tips."

"You're welcome. Let's get the bikes to the shop and you folks to your cars."

Technically, their excursion wasn't over until the bikes

were checked in, but she told them she'd handle it and let them go find Peter. She had their cell numbers in the paperwork if she needed anything.

Peter's bike wasn't trashed exactly, but one of the hand brakes was popped for sure, the front wheel was definitely bent, and the handlebars needed adjusting. She parked the other bikes, left that one in the driveway, and went inside.

"Hey, girl. You park the bikes for me?" Isley had gotten some sun and had a healthy glow today.

"Yep. You're going to want to have a look at one of them, though."

"Okay, just tag it and let me know what needs adjusting."

"I think you're going to want to come see it. Like, before I go." Frankie gave her a sheepish shrug.

Isley glanced over, and Merida, the mechanic, appeared from the back, walked past her, and went outside. After a few quiet moments of turning her head this way and that, she sighed.

"ER?"

Frankie nodded. "By ambulance. EMT extraction on the trail."

"Damn. Head?"

"Arm. Definitely broken."

"The frame seems okay. Brakes are a pain in the ass, and it needs a new front wheel...I mean, if you're gonna break it, might as well do it right, huh?"

"I don't think the guy was screwing around, he just zigged when he should have zagged or something, you know? I am so sorry about the bike."

"No worries. Job security." Merida winked at her, red hair glowing in the late afternoon sun. The look on Frankie's face must have given away exactly how she was feeling because Merida straightened up and caught her eye. "Really. Renters bust these things up all the time. I got this, okay? No worries. You have a good night."

"Yeah? Okay. You too. Thanks again." She went to her car, dug out a bottle of water, and got moving.

She was nearly downtown before she realized she'd missed the turnoff to head up to M&M. She thought about turning around but changed her mind when she saw someone come out of Cherry's Pies with a pizza to go. That was a great idea, she needed some company, and Lucy told her lots of the M&M folks hung out there after work. She could go for a slice of pizza too.

The smell of hot cheese and garlic washed over her as she went inside and made her stomach growl. Cherry's was one of many buildings in town that had carefully preserved its frontier town look. The false-front façade was exactly that, and the inside had a retro-diner kind of feel with the bar and some booths in the main room and smaller dining rooms off to the side.

"Need a table, honey?" a hostess asked as she approached a solid, round reception stand. Her name tag said, "Linda."

"I just want a slice. Can I sit at the bar?"

"Help yourself."

"Thanks." She wandered in, taking in the signs on the walls and all the wood decor. The place had that rockabilly feel but so different than back east where everything was chrome and shiny. Chunky, natural wood walls replaced the tinted glass windows you'd see at home, and the bar was solid and carved instead of rimmed with shiny aluminum and topped with bright white laminate.

But it was clearly the same era, and she felt completely comfortable finding herself a fake-leather upholstered stool at the bar.

"What can I get you?" The bartender was over instantly,

smiling, flashing white teeth, and sporting a too-tight black polo, which seemed to be the uniform.

"Can I get a slice of—"

"Get her the pepperoni and green chili special, Chuck."

She and the bartender looked toward the other end of the bar, and Patrick gave her a wave.

"Hey!" She waved back and winked at Chuck. "I'll have an IPA too, please. Whatever is on tap."

"You got it."

"Thanks." She got up and moved down to Patrick, who was already into one of two huge slices of pizza. "Is that what you ordered me?"

"It is. You haven't lived until you've tried it."

"Well, I am into living so…" She climbed onto a barstool, shaking her head. "These were not made for short people. How are you?"

"I'm good. You? Are you coming from work? You look it."

She knew it too. She was dusty and probably had awful helmet-head, but half the people in here were equally dusty or mud-covered and touched by the mountain sunshine. "I am. It's my first weekend, and it was a very long day."

"I bet you're tired. How did it go?"

She glanced at Patrick, trying to decide whether or not to tell the truth.

"Frankie! You survived." Lucy had great timing.

"Hey, there." She grinned as Lucy came over. "Come sit. I'm having…green chili and—what?"

"Pepperoni." Lucy and Patrick said together.

Lucy nodded. "So good."

"Patrick, this is Lucy. I work and live with her up at M and M. Lucy, this is Patrick Young, Pen—uh, Aspen's brother."

"Aspen?" Lucy raised an eyebrow.

"Penny."

"Oh. Hey, Patrick. Nice to meet you." Lucy reached over her and they shook hands.

"Penny, wow. We haven't called her Penny since college. When she came back from Vermont she told us she wanted to use her real name."

She shrugged. "I've just always known her as Penny. Hard habit to break, but I'm trying." Kind of. If Patrick had switched, though, she'd better try harder.

"So...about that. Heather told me that you knew her before dinner at the house."

She nodded to Patrick. "I figured you knew by now."

The bartender set her beer down and after Lucy ordered, she pushed it closer. "You're going to want that."

Frankie rolled her eyes. "Gee. Thanks." She took a big swig, not sure how thrilled she was about these worlds colliding unexpectedly.

Patrick looked between them. "Nobody told me your story, just that you used to be together. So, fill me in on what I'm missing."

She didn't know how much Penny would want him to know, so she didn't get into details. "Aspen and I went to school together."

"In Vermont?"

She nodded. "UVM. Rally the Catamount."

"What exactly is a catamount?" Lucy asked.

"It's extinct."

"So, wait. Are you—"

"Yeah. I'm the one that—you know."

It was Patrick's turn to stare. "That was you?"

She nodded. "Yeah. Unfortunately."

"Oh, man. Was she upset about you. She used some colorful language once she finally got out of bed."

Dammit. This talk on Monday was going to be so hard. "Fuck."

"Sorry. But it's true. You're pretty brave coming back here. Ballsy."

"That's my middle name, might as well live up to it."

"Wait, did you know I was her brother?"

"Not on the ride, but I figured it out in the parking lot when you took your helmet off, and Heather said your name was Young." She wasn't going to lie; she'd take her lumps now and be honest. The last thing she needed was for Patrick and Aspen to compare stories and catch her fibbing.

Patrick's eyes went wide. "Damn." He took a bite of his pizza and shook his head. "So when we invited you to dinner—"

"Yeah."

Lucy slapped her hand on the bar. "She totally knew. We knew. She talks about Penny—or, Aspen—all the time."

She chuckled, embarrassed. "Gosh, I'm so glad we all ran into each other."

Patrick laughed. "Hey, it's your funeral. I want Aspen to be happy. If that's your angle, then great." His eyes narrowed and he caught her eye. "But if you hurt her, you'll never work in this town again. Got me?"

Oh, shit. He was a good little brother. She swallowed hard. "I got you. I won't."

Patrick's glare dissolved and he laughed again. "I'm kidding. Some. Mostly. If you're back for her, don't fuck it up, though, she loved you."

Lucy whistled. "This is better than color TV."

Their pizza arrived, and Frankie was relieved by the interruption. Lucy had ordered the same thing, but Chuck put down a margarita instead of a beer.

"Ooh. This looks so good." It was huge, so she was glad for the knife and fork.

Before she dug in, she put a hand on Patrick's shoulder. "No joke, Patrick. I blew it, it was all me. I had reasons. Good ones at the time, but I didn't handle it all well, obviously. And I've missed her. I'm going to fix it, explain…Monday, in fact. We have a date. And then I'm going to make her fall back in love with me."

"Okay. People fuck up. It happens." Patrick grinned at her. "Good luck. She's a stubborn pain in the ass. But I like you."

"Thanks." She nodded. "Yeah. That hasn't changed. I kind of love that about her."

"Me too." Patrick picked up his beer. "To the pain in the ass."

She and Lucy lifted their glasses and clinked them together. "Here, here."

"Okay. Let me try this." Frankie took a big bite of her pizza. Her mouth filled with tangy pepperoni, spicy chilies, and rich cheese, and she moaned happily. "*Oh. Mmm.* Good call."

"See? Always ask a local what to order."

Lucy snorted. "Unless they say Hawaiian."

Frankie rolled her eyes. She liked Hawaiian too.

"Hey, so how was your first day?" Lucy dug into her pizza, cutting a bite off the end. "Was it awesome? Did you have fun?"

"It was…" *Oh, Lord. Well, here goes nothing.* "The morning ride was fantastic. Bright sun, great trail, and the people I was taking down it were really technical and wanted to know all the good spots. It was great."

"Awesome. That's how you start a new job. And your afternoon group?"

She puffed out a breath between her lips. "Well. That one ended with an ambulance ride."

Both Patrick and Lucy froze midbite.

"Oh, shit." Lucy's eyes went wide.

Patrick picked up his beer. "Was it bad?"

"Broken arm. He won't be riding for a while. It could have

been worse. He wrecked the bike too."

"Damn."

"Yeah, and the thing is, I was on my own with them because they signed up as experienced. And they were mostly, but they were young and...I don't know." She stared into her beer glass. "I didn't see what happened; he was behind me. There are always risks, I know, and his friends say he looked fine one second, and then his front wheel twisted and he was off his bike just like that."

"Well, it's not like it's your fault, Frankie."

"No, but you know how it is. I was responsible up there. His friends were a little wigged out."

"Which trail?" Patrick asked. "I've wiped out on all of them."

"Yeah?" That made her smile a little. Patrick was a good guy. "I don't know what the locals call it. It was nine-twenty-five."

"Oh, that's a good one. Tough but fun. That bit between the boulders can be unforgiving."

"It was right after that, actually. I had to hike up and close the trail at the fork above it."

Patrick nodded. "People sometimes have too much speed where the trail opens up. They think they're past the hardest part but they're not."

"Right? And I told them to check their speed when we stopped at the fork before that section just for that reason."

"Well, then he either didn't listen, or his wheel just caught something. It was probably just a fluke thing, Frankie. We all know accidents can happen."

Lucy nodded. "You folks wear all that gear for a reason."

That was true. They didn't just rent helmets. They wore chest armor and elbow and knee pads. Her own protective gear had a few dings too. And it seemed like she was always replacing something.

"You're good, I promise. If you're worried, you go talk to Lupe. She'll tell you. Accidents happen. We do everything we can, and people still have accidents."

"That bike, though."

"The contracts cover damage, stop worrying. Seriously. Talk to Lupe."

"I might. I probably should, huh? So the owners know? So they hear it from me." And it really might help for someone higher up to tell her it was all good.

Lucy nodded. "Couldn't hurt."

"I am so glad I decided I needed a beer and some pizza tonight."

"Me too. I got the scoop on you and my sister." Patrick teased.

"I gave you no scoop. Nothing scoopy. Do not tell her I gave you any scoop. Facts yes, scoops? No." Lord, that would be all she needed.

Patrick and Lucy laughed at her.

"Eat your pizza and quit stressing it. By the end of the summer, you'll be way more chill." Lucy looked at her. "Not chill that people get hurt, chill that it's not your fault."

"Unless it is," Patrick chimed in helpfully. She glared at him and he winked back.

"Y'all want to move to a booth? I want another beer and maybe another slice."

"Yeah. Let's do it."

"Chuck, we're relocating over there." Lucy pointed to one of the booths along the wall opposite the bar.

"You got it. Get comfy."

They settled up their bar check, left a nice tip, then picked up their food and moved to the booth so they could talk and eat more easily than at the bar.

This really was a great idea.

Maybe she wasn't such a fuckup after all.

CHAPTER 12

"*O*h my God, Roz. What did you do to yourself?"

Aspen looked up as Minnie dashed across the room. Roz, the co-op's only jewelry artist, was making her way into the studio on crutches. Her rainbow dreads were as wild and woolly as ever, but her usual enormous smile was sheepish and she was rolling her eyes.

"I had family in town and we decided to go have some fun."

"Well, why the hell would you do that?" Damon hurried over and took Roz's bag, laughing.

Minnie walked alongside Roz as she made her way to her station. "Were you sober?"

Roz's eyes went wide at the teasing. "We were rafting. We went on one of those M and M rafting things."

"Oh, you killed your knee rafting? That sucks."

"Nope. I killed my knee getting out of the raft *after* we were done." Roz sat with a groan. "This is me we're talking about."

"At least it wasn't your wrist like last summer." Aspen got up and went over for a hug.

Damon snorted. "Or your broken rib over the winter."

"Fractured, thank you. From coughing."

"Right, the rib." Aspen headed back to her own table. Roz was being well looked after. "You should have made up a better story."

"Mugger."

"A mob shakedown."

"MMA?"

"Werewolves."

"Oh, I like that one." Roz's eyes went wide. "Dragging me to the roof of my building during a full moon to make me one of their own."

"I've heard crazier things. Aspen has a girlfriend."

"What?"

Aspen blinked. "Damon, go to your station." She pointed toward his huge water fountain sculpture that was coming along beautifully. Everyone laughed as Damon slunk away, giggling.

"You have a—"

"After the meeting, Roz." Aspen winked. She had no intention of saying anything at all after the meeting. She wasn't sure anyone would be speaking to her at that point anyway. "Do we have everyone?"

Minnie handed her a sign-in sheet. "Everyone but Grace. Her granddaughter was born this morning. She'll call you tomorrow."

"Oh, wonderful. Good for her." Aspen looked at her, and Minnie must have seen the slightly terrified look in her eyes.

"You've got this. Just like we talked about at lunch, right? Honest. Humble. The whole truth."

She nodded. She was very much on board with that plan, but that didn't mean she wasn't nervous.

She watched for a minute, taking in all the faces, bodies, complexions, and ages in the room. One of the best things about this group was its diversity; it was a big part of what drew her to these folks. Broad-minded, creative, local people. She stayed standing in front of her table and waved a hand to get their attention. "Hey, everyone. Before I start, we're only together like this once a month, so I want you all to take a look around and give a little smile and a hello to someone you haven't seen since the last meeting. This place is only as strong as its members, and all of you are important and appreciated."

She had seen everyone at some point, but she gave them all a wave anyway. This was going to be a tough meeting.

"Okay." She waited for the room to get quiet again. "Thanks. So…we have some real business to discuss this meeting, and like last winter, it's a mix of good news and bad news. So I'm going to talk, and I need you just to listen to the whole thing even though I know you're going to have tons of questions. You need to see the big picture first, and then we'll talk details, okay? I'll take questions, and we'll make it a discussion after I'm done."

"That sounds ominous." Damon pulled up a stool and sat.

"Some of it is, yeah." She nodded. "Okay, so, as you may already know, the all-inclusive deals up at the resort this winter have taken a real toll on the whole town…"

She laid out their financial situation as clearly as she knew how, and she explained about the budget, her salary, the rent, and everything else. She could feel the quiet dread settle into the room where there was usually a lot of lively discussion. Everyone let her get all the way through it, though, just as she'd asked. She took another deep breath when she finished and looked around the room.

"I'm sorry, everyone. I should have told you last month, but I honestly believed things would improve. I promise I'm doing the best I can, but I know I've let you down. I didn't prepare for a dry spell of this magnitude in the budget, and like Bucky told me, I didn't understand how much—"

"Aspen," Minnie said softly, interrupting her. "I know you wanted us to wait until you were done, but I think I've heard enough. Bottom line as far as I am concerned—we've all been paid. You took the financial hit on yourself. That's taking responsibility if you ask me, not that this situation is anyone's fault. You said it at the beginning; almost everyone in town that relies on seasonal money is feeling it. We probably should have expected this, you know?"

Aspen puffed out a breath. She knew not everyone would feel that way, but she appreciated Minnie stepping in on her side. "Thanks, Minnie. Before I finish, in addition to having the best landlord in town, I do have some good news."

"We could use some, Aspen."

"Will it save the studio?"

"Hush up, everyone," Damon suggested gently. "Let her finish."

She looked around the room and continued. "A couple of months ago, I called Jed Brightlow, the guest relations manager up at Pines Peak, to talk to him about putting some of our work in their gift shops. Not only did he finally return my call, but he came down last week to see the gallery and all of your work in person, and he agreed that local representation would be good for us both. I signed a contract to put our pieces in all three of their gift shops beginning next month."

The mood in the room lifted slightly, and the little buzz of approval made her feel better. "So this is going to take some planning. Jed says each shop has a different vibe and price point, so I wanted to ask for some volunteers to go up there with me to scope them out and help me decide what kind of work to put in each of them."

Roz's hand went right up. "I am all over that."

"Oh, that would be great, Roz. Thank you." Roz was the

founder of the co-op long before it had a studio or a gallery. She was local and knew everyone's work, she was the perfect choice, and regardless of who else volunteered, Aspen would have asked for Roz's help anyway. "Anyone else?"

Sophia's hand went up timidly. "I'd be willing to help, but I don't know if—"

"You'd be perfect, honey." Roz nodded to her. "Young eyes are just what we need."

It was true, actually. Sophia made many of the handcrafts in the shop—soaps and candles, scarves and woven bowls, even hard candies. Things that would sell well in a gift shop.

Sophia smiled. "Great. Thanks."

"Do we have flyers or postcards or anything? You know, advertising?"

She shook her head. "I have a business card. That's it."

"I'll design something. That's my day job, you know. And I have an in with a printer."

"Max. Thank you." Why hadn't she thought about that earlier? "That would be amazing."

Brandy's hand went up. "My dad is a retired accountant. He's bored as hell. Do you think he could help?"

"Oh. Yes, definitely." She'd been doing it all herself.

"Are you going to raise our dues? What about the cut that the gallery takes? And these gift shops?"

Shit. The answer was yes, but she hadn't gotten to that bad news yet.

"Hey, y'all." Damon cleared his throat and the room went quiet. "You should, Aspen."

"Should...?"

"You should raise our co-op dues and take a bigger cut. It's reasonable. We all need to help save this place."

"We haven't had an increase in dues since you started the gallery," Roz added. "We've never had a need. Now, there's obviously a need."

"I...I was getting to that, and I was going to ask. Thank you, Damon." She scanned the room. "If raising dues and increasing the gallery's commission presents a hardship to anyone, please come see me privately and we'll talk and work something out. I have no interest in pricing anyone out of the co-op. You were all here before me, and you all work too hard. I'll have a proposal out this week with the new numbers and a date for a special meeting to approve them."

She took yet another deep breath. "I was very nervous about this meeting. I'm so proud to be a part of all of this. My door is always open, okay? Anything you want to talk about. Come in, call me, email me, text me...you're each incredibly important to the energy and the balance of this whole thing."

"Have you folks seen the *saké* set Aspen just finished?" Minnie came over to her station, picked up her *saké* bottle, showing it around. "Look at this. It's porcelain. Isn't it gorgeous?"

The praise from her fellow artists made her blush, and Minnie's thoughtfulness made her a little emotional. Traditionally, they ended their monthly meetings by admiring what everyone was up to, and Minnie had just effectively ended the business discussion for the night. Aspen was incredibly grateful for the intervention.

She walked over to Sophia's table to admire a scarf Sophia had felted, feeling like she would sleep much better tonight. They were going to be okay.

CHAPTER 13

"*I* thought you were going on a hike?"

"I am." Frankie peered out the cabin window, then went to find her sneakers.

"In sneakers and shorts?" Alex followed her.

"Well, it's more of a stroll."

"A stroll? You don't stroll."

"No, but…she does."

"She? Oh, you mean Penny."

"Yes. No, Aspen." *Dammit.* She was trying.

"She changed her name too?"

"No, that's her real name. Penny for short. She used to think living in Colorado and being called Aspen was weird." She got her shoes on and went looking for her water bottle. Alex followed her again.

"And…it's not weird now?"

"I don't know. What does it matter? Why are you asking so many questions? Where is my fucking water bottle?"

Alex silently pointed right to it.

"Thank you."

"You're a little stressed, honey."

"I'm not stressed, I'm nervous as fuck. All right, and stressed. Yes. Okay? We have to have a talk, you know? *The* talk. And I've been thinking about it, and I was stupid, and she's not going to understand and—fuck, I don't want to blow this."

"Are you sorry?"

She stared at Alex. "What? Of course."

"No, I mean *for real* sorry. Do you regret it? Do you wish you'd done something differently?"

She sighed. She wished she'd done some things differently. Stayed in touch, for one. But she'd felt so trapped at first, and then she'd let so much time go by it had been too awkward to make the call. "Yes. Big time."

"Okay, then. Good. That's the best you can do, you know? Be honest."

Honest was the plan for the day. For the week. Honest was going to be her plan for the next hundred years.

A horn honked lightly outside as she was screwing the top on her water bottle, and she jumped. *Fuck.*

"She's getting out of the car. Ooh, that's Penny?" Alex was staring out the window. "Damn, girl, no wonder you hauled your butt all the way out here."

"I know. Oh, God."

"Hey. Breathe." Alex took her by the shoulders and walked her through a deep breath, letting it out slowly. "You've got this. Frankie. You're adorable too."

Penny knocked on the door and Alex winked at her "Enjoy your stroll."

"Thanks." She stood there, frozen for a second.

"Are you going to get the door?"

"Shit. Right." She laughed, which sounded strange to her own ears, and went to the door.

"Good morning."

Aspen's smile was so beautiful it nearly made her forget her nerves. "Good morning."

"Are you ready? Am I dressed all right? I have boots in the trunk but I thought—"

She chuckled at that. "You said 'stroll.' I have sneakers. You look great, by the way. I love that top."

"Yeah? Thank you. It's hard to know how to dress for a date that's a stroll and a big talk." There wasn't a bit of sarcasm in that statement, just a little humor, and Penny seemed nervous too, which was odd because she hadn't done a thing.

"Right? Do I wear the pink tank top to apologize or the understated blue one?" She winked.

"I see you went for blue. I brought lunch. I thought maybe a picnic?"

"That sounds great."

"Hi. I'm Alex." Alex peered over her shoulder. "Get along now, lovebirds, you're letting the flies in."

"Hi, Alex. Nice to meet you." Penny winked. "I'll get her out of your hair."

"Oh, please do. It's my day off too, you know."

Frankie laughed and stepped out of the doorway and onto the little porch. "See you later."

"I hope not." Alex winked and closed the door.

She shook her head and followed Penny to the car. "Sorry about that."

"Alex seems nice."

"They are. Sarcastic, funny, and very…sweet. Kind. I live with good people."

"I've never been up here before, you know that? I've never made friends with the seasonal people." Penny glanced over at her. "That sounded snooty, but I don't mean it like that. I'm just not outdoorsy, and our paths never cross in a way that—"

She laughed. "It wasn't snooty. I understand. Most of us seasonal folks are here to work, and we kind of keep to ourselves because we're busy and we all live together. I get it."

"Oh. Good. Anyway, it's nice up here. The cabins are cute. How many roommates do you have?"

"Three." She loved that Penny was asking, taking an interest. "Alex is one, Lucy and Milo are the other two. Milo has been coming here for years, and he's like the cabin dad. He's not even really seasonal—he works with the horses on the ranch, and I think that might be year-round." She should ask him. But she hadn't allowed herself to think beyond the end of the summer yet.

"Right. Lucy is the one Patrick met at Cherry's?"

"Yep." *Oh, boy.* Patrick had tattled. She wondered how much he'd said. "It was neat to run into him. We actually have a lot in common. He's a nice guy."

"He's an annoying little brother." Penny glanced at her, then back at the road. "And a nice guy."

They laughed, and Penny turned on the radio, keeping it low background noise. "I figured we'd hit the preserve? You spend so much time on the mountain, I thought it would be a nice change of scenery. It's pretty this time of year."

"That's a great idea. I haven't been there yet."

"It's less exciting I guess, but there's lots of grass and birds and flowers...fewer people, especially on a Monday. Places to picnic." Penny shrugged. "I walk there a lot."

She nodded. Penny was taking her to her space. That was interesting. Probably good.

"Sounds nice."

"I'm learning to ride again, and we go there sometimes too."

"Yeah?" What did learning again mean? "Did you forget how?"

Penny laughed. "No, I just…I was good in high school. I want to be good again."

"What does good mean?" The last time Frankie had ridden a horse, she'd just sat on it and rode. "You mean competing?"

"Maybe eventually, yeah."

"Like, barrel racing?"

"No. That's awesome too, and I did it in high school some, but no. My parents taught me to ride English, and I was into dressage. I'm trying to build up those skills again."

"Oh, wow."

"I literally just started back a month ago. I only ride once a week right now. It's hard to find the time, for one thing, and also lessons can be expensive."

Right. And Penny said she hadn't paid herself in two months. "You want to own a horse someday?"

"We already do. Patrick and I own two, actually. We've leased them to the barn since we don't ride often. They belonged to my parents. Patrick set up the leases when Mom couldn't ride anymore." Penny pulled into a small, gravel parking lot. They were the only car in it. "We're here."

"Cool." Frankie got out and looked around. It was very green on the other side of the split rail fence that ran along one side of the lot, and there was a paved path that disappeared into some trees at the one end. "Wow. It's so quiet."

"Are the mountains not quiet?"

"Bikes aren't quiet. Riders aren't really either." The trails never felt this relaxed. They always felt in motion somehow. Challenging.

Penny grabbed a cooler and slung it over her shoulder. "I like how still it is here. There are a couple of places I like to sit where time almost stops. It sounds weird I guess, but I'll show you."

"Sounds nice. Time kind of flies for me. I don't think

about it much, but when I do it's like *whoa*, how is it summer? How am I twenty-five?"

"I can't believe it's been two years since..." Penny sighed.

She took a breath. "Mm. Okay. Is that my cue?"

"Sorry. No. I mean, we do need to talk, right? But I didn't mean that like—" Penny took her hand and squeezed it. "Sorry."

She nodded and held on, that firm grip making her brave. "I've been worrying about talking to you since before I drove out here. The thing is, it's not a huge long explanation, it's pretty simple, I just—well. I want to be honest like I should have been back then."

They stepped onto the little paved path. It was surrounded by thick trees and as they walked it felt like the world disappeared. There was nothing to see but bark and leaves. And Penny.

"I'm ready to listen. I wasn't then, but I am now. I certainly am today."

"Okay." She could feel her palm start to sweat in Penny's but Penny didn't let go. She started speaking slowly. "I should have called you. That morning, later that day, I just...I don't even know why I didn't, exactly. I was afraid, ashamed. Something. I couldn't do what I told you I would do—what you wanted me to do."

She remembered that night so well. She relived it a lot, worrying over what she'd done and hadn't done. "I drove to my parents' house for dinner that night like I said I would, to tell them I was going with you. And why. To finally come out to them and damn the consequences like we talked about, right? I was ready to move on, I wanted to go." She watched Penny, working through the knot in her stomach. "I was so in love with you."

She still was.

Penny held her gaze for just a second and glanced away. "And then what?"

"And then the world disappeared from under my feet. I got there...Mom was making dinner, but the house was a mess and she looked like hell. And Dad wasn't there at all. I was so confused."

"He wasn't there?" Penny frowned at her.

"It's a very long story, Penny, but the bottom line is that Mom had been diagnosed with brain cancer, and Dad..." She shook her head. She'd never been able to understand it. "He'd left her. He found out she was sick and he *left* her."

"What?"

"He moved out. He was gone and she didn't even know where he went. I mean, I don't think she wanted to know, honestly. She said he didn't want to deal with it, but that was all she would ever tell me. She wasn't even upset. She seemed kind of relieved, actually, but she was alone. She was trying to deal with the cancer all by herself."

"Jesus."

"She hadn't told me. She hadn't told a lot of people, as it turned out. If I'd gone with you, left Vermont without going to see them, I might not ever have known." Her parents were very vocal about "the gays" and talked often about how their friend's son had "gone to therapy for it" like it was some disease. She'd never come out to them, obviously. She'd left for college and hadn't looked back.

Until Penny asked her to. Penny had wanted her to tell the truth and close that door—if she had to. And she would have had to.

But.

"I couldn't leave her alone, and I couldn't come out to her at that point either. A big part of me wanted to leave too; it's not like we were close. But...she was alone, you know?"

Penny stopped walking and stared at her. "I don't understand. You couldn't at least show up and tell me? Text me before the plane took off? Something? Did you think I wouldn't get it?"

"I know, I know. At the time I was…you said you couldn't be with someone that was still in the closet. You *said*…you made me promise, remember? To tell my folks. Tell them, and then I could get on the plane with you."

"Frankie…but I didn't mean…"

"Yeah. I know that now. It's something I thought about a lot—where I was then emotionally and where I am now. At the time, though, I believed you. You were serious enough to make me promise. And by the time I grew up enough to understand…" She'd called Penny exactly once and the call hadn't gone through.

She never got the nerve up to call again.

Part of her had been devastated and part of her relieved. She hadn't looked very hard for a new number.

"Oh, shit." Penny started walking again. "*Shit*. Fuck, Frankie. I was so upset at the time—I was angry at you. I changed my number."

She nodded. "Yeah. I figured. And I knew you were probably angry, but I was clueless about cancer and overwhelmed, and…it was a bad year. After the first six or eight months, I barely recognized her, and I tried to take care of her at home as long as I could after that but she sometimes had no idea who I was and—God, it was awful."

"Frankie, I'm…I don't know what to say. I'm so sorry you had to go through that."

"I just…after she died, I was dealing with all of this guilt and I didn't have, I don't know…for a while I didn't have the will or the energy to track you down." She'd felt like she should have missed her mother more than she did. She still struggled with that sometimes. "And I figured you were doing exactly what you said you were going to do. Following your dream, opening a gallery. Making art. Good things. I wanted good things for you."

They walked for a while silently, each lost in their own thoughts and that seemed okay. Penny needed a minute. Hell, she needed to breathe too. But when Penny finally took her hand again, Frankie stopped them to catch Penny's eyes. "I'm really sorry. Honestly. I still have no idea where my dad went or why—I don't even care at this point—and I never actually came out to Mom." She felt the tears falling and swiped at them, but they just kept coming.

"Frankie." Penny's arms slipped around her and pulled her in. "It's okay. Let it go."

"What?" She tried to pull away reflexively, but Penny just hugged her harder.

"I feel awful. I had no idea, obviously, but I—"

"It's not your fault. It's mine. It's all mine. I did this to us. I broke your heart. This is all on me."

"I'm sorry, too. Yes, I wanted you to come out to your parents. I did. They were this heavy obstacle for you, hanging over your head and your life, and I thought it would be good for you to tell them. I thought you should find out once and for all where they stood and be done with them before you moved away with me. Like...closure. It was a tough-love thing, I guess, but it wasn't the kind of ultimatum you thought it was. I didn't mean I wouldn't...Frankie, I'm so sorry."

Her mind was swimming with so many thoughts and emotions, she felt dizzy with it all. She heard everything Penny had just said, but it was taking a while to sink in. It was hard to chalk two years of guilt and shame up to a series of crazy mistakes, but that was what this was starting to feel like. She needed to say something, anything, so Penny would know she heard her, but she didn't find the words before Penny burst into tears too.

She was glad for the isolation, the deserted path, and the thick trees as they stood there together, holding on tight and emptying themselves of two years of frustrated, angry, lonely, brokenhearted tears.

She'd never felt so raw, so relieved. Or so in love.

They seemed to recover together, putting a couple of inches of space between them so they could breathe. She looked into Penny's deep, dark eyes, seeing everything, and made sure to let Penny in too.

"I love you." Her voice sounded rough in her own ears as she spoke.

Penny nodded. "I love you, too. This is a fucking mess, but we—"

"Was. It was a mess. Now it's going to be beautiful." She kissed Penny and Penny fell right into it. She could taste the salty tears, but they were mixed with something much sweeter. Penny wasn't holding anything back anymore, her kiss was simple and generous. It wasn't hungry or needy, just free. Honest. Their kiss was everything it had always been.

Just love.

CHAPTER 14

*A*spen stared up at the blue sky, watching a fluffy white cloud slowly make its way from left to right, changing shape as it went along—one minute a round little pig, the next a creepy face with an eye patch. It looked like an alligator head at the moment, opening to eat some other unsuspecting cloud animal.

She had an arm around Frankie, who rested on her shoulder after a naughty little quickie with their hands down each other's shorts in this pasture in the middle of nowhere. They hadn't seen a soul since they parked this morning. Not a rider on horseback, no hikers, not even a lone jogger. She doubted anyone had seen them either, but they'd never know.

She felt better and worse after the talk that brought that awful set of misunderstandings and mistakes out in the open, but relieved in any case—and hopeful too.

Now it's going to be beautiful.

That was enough. Whatever they'd been through, whatever Frankie had been dealing with, their feelings were real and strong and there was only one way to go now. Forward.

"Mm." Frankie hummed, nuzzling against her breast. "I can hear you thinking."

"I'm watching the clouds."

"Cloud, you mean? It looks like a turtle." Frankie sounded muzzy, relaxed.

"It was an alligator a second ago."

"I think I fell asleep."

"We both did." She kissed Frankie's forehead. "You want lunch?"

"In a minute. I'm too comfy."

She agreed. This was nice, just lying here, glowing a bit, with nowhere to be. "You do feel good."

"Remember the time we almost got caught in that park in Stowe?"

"Yes, I left my favorite bra behind."

Frankie laughed. "I had tree bark burns on my ass."

She shook her head, chuckling softly. "Yeah well, they were funny. And they went away, but I never got my bra back."

"What did you bring for lunch?"

"Chicken salad. And beer."

Frankie sat up on one elbow. "Oh. I could so go for a beer."

"Just one each, but I had this feeling…"

"Yeah, good call." Frankie sat the rest of the way up and stretched, then gave those blond braids a tug. "You're pretty."

"Hm." She didn't feel pretty. Her eyes still felt puffy, and she was sure she had mascara all over her face. "Pretty like a raccoon?"

"A little." Frankie chuckled. "It's sexy, though."

"I should have known," she said as she also sat up. She ran her fingers through her hair and put it up in what was probably an un-stylish messy bun with a scrunchie she had in her pocket. She winked at Frankie. "I mean, who wears mascara to a Big Talk?"

"You. You wear mascara to a hair-of-the-dog breakfast."

"I did. And everyone made fun of me."

Frankie ran gentle thumbs under her eyes, clearing the makeup. "Didn't stop you from doing it again."

"Nope."

"That's a little better."

"Yeah?"

Frankie shrugged. "You're hot either way."

"Dork." She dragged the cooler over and opened it. "So… do we need to talk about anything else?"

"Not unless it's about me spending the night at your house tonight and buying you a boozy brunch tomorrow."

"Yes, on the first part, but a firm maybe on the second. I have champagne, and you haven't had breakfast on my deck yet."

"Okay. Good talk." Frankie kissed her cheek.

She smiled as she found the bottle opener and opened their beers. More would come up over time. She'd ask for some details about Frankie's mom and share a little about the cancer that had taken her own mother from her too. But today had been enough. More than enough for them both.

"Oh. Kaiser rolls. Is this your chicken salad too?" Frankie pulled the sandwiches out, turning one around to see. "Looks like it."

"Yes. I remembered how much you used to like it."

"I don't really eat anyone else's. There's usually too much mayo."

She nodded knowingly. "You like the mustard in mine."

"I knew it was something." Frankie winked at her and held up her beer. "To a beautiful day."

"To a beautiful day." She clinked and they both sipped,

then opened up their sandwiches. "So, what did you do to your knee?"

Frankie looked at it and sighed. "Oh. I slipped on the trail. Got a little scuffed up. No big deal."

"On your first day?"

"Oh. No, this was on my own. My first day was a whole other disaster."

"Oh, no." She shifted to face Frankie more squarely. "What happened?"

Frankie sighed, sounding embarrassed. "A kid in my afternoon group wiped out and broke his arm. I had to call the trail service EMTs to come pick him up. Nobody is saying it was my fault or that I did anything wrong, but man. I feel responsible anyway, you know? His friends were kind of wigged out too. It was a wild end to the day."

Aspen was willing to bet no one was upset with Frankie at all. Careening down a steep hill on a narrow path just wasn't safe. Patrick had been injured numerous times himself. "Wow. Started off with a bang, huh?"

"Shut up." Frankie laughed though and didn't seem upset. "I had my own little freak-out, but my roomies talked me out of it."

"People get hurt doing what you do, I guess."

"Sure. Even if you do everything right and take every precaution, accidents happen. I've had a few good ones myself, as you know."

"Your arm..." Frankie broke her right arm in two places the summer before senior year. She'd even needed surgery.

"I had to learn to make you come left-handed." Frankie waggled her eyebrows. "I have some serious ambidextrous skills now."

Aspen felt her face flush and her cheeks heat up. "Too bad you can't put that on your résumé."

"Right? Dictation software wasn't going to help me with

that at all." Frankie cracked up. Aspen loved the easy sound of it and the way it lit up Frankie's blue eyes.

"I love your smile."

Frankie blushed, hiding behind her sandwich by taking a big bite. "*Mm. M-m-m.*"

They ate for a bit, and Frankie proved she really was hungry. The first half of the sandwich disappeared quickly. "Where are things with the co-op? Did you talk to anyone?"

"Everyone. We had a meeting. It went very, very well."

"Yeah?" There was that smile again. The support felt good, and Frankie looked so genuinely pleased for her.

"They hardly even let me apologize. And then people pitched in ideas and volunteered to help with the resort contract. They brought up higher dues before I could. It was amazing."

"They sound like such a great group. I can't wait to meet them; I want to come visit the gallery." Frankie leaned close. "Like the actual gallery, not just your office."

"Ha-ha. Yes. Please come and I'll show you everything. You can meet whoever is working in the studio. I'd love that."

"Have you thought about a fund raiser?"

She blinked at Frankie. "Like a charity thing?"

"Well? More like a…gallery night. Or an exhibition. You know, fancy with wine, an admission fee, inflated prices, and artists talking about their work. Like a…"

"Gala." A gala. A fund-raising gala. Frankie was on to something.

"Right. A gala. A community thing. Something to make money to support the gallery. Advertise all over, even up at Pines Peak. Why not?"

"I love that idea. We could have it…maybe in the studio?" The wheels were turning now. She loved a party anyway, and one to benefit the artists could be so much fun.

"Or at your house. I mean, that deck…that view."

She nodded, already thinking food, wine, invitations… "Frankie. You're a genius. We could totally do this."

"Sure, just let me know how I can help."

"You want to help? When I said 'we,' I meant the co-op members, but I…I'd love that."

"It would be fun. I'm also a bartender, remember. If you need a volunteer."

"Oh, my God. I forgot." That was how Frankie had put herself through school. Scholarships, work-study, and bartending.

"The literature degree hasn't helped me much yet, but the bartending is a handy skill that gets the rent paid." Frankie finished the last bite of her sandwich. "*Mm.*"

"I'm going to ask everyone. See what they think." Maybe a silent auction, some local entertainment. Even if it wasn't a huge moneymaker, it would be a fantastic visibility thing.

Frankie sipped her beer. "We always were a good team, Penny."

She knew she should correct Frankie. She'd gone by Aspen since she moved back home, had decided she preferred it, and even Patrick had understood and made the switch for her. But there was so much affection in the way Frankie said her nickname, she wasn't sure she wanted to.

She actually liked it.

Their talk changed everything. There was no blame anymore, no anger. Probably a lot of regret, but Frankie didn't seem interested in dwelling on that, and Aspen was totally on board.

And she was pleasantly surprised by how interested Frankie was in the gallery and her work. Maybe she shouldn't be; Frankie had always been supportive, had always liked her pottery and encouraged her ideas, had always understood her goals. It was just…it felt good to have someone not related to her so firmly in her corner.

Frankie's goals were less clear. She'd never had a "when I grow up" story, but she loved the outdoors and sports in general, and Aspen thought Frankie had found a good niche for herself.

It was going to be good. This was a solid thing, now. Real. She loved Frankie.

She loved all of it.

CHAPTER 15

*F*rankie had always loved the mountains; she was born and raised in the Green Mountains of Vermont. She loved the sky from the top of a ski lift, the view of mountain peaks from the valley in October, and the way that the sun would set, making those same peaks look like they were on fire. Vermont was her first love. But summer in the Rockies was spectacular.

It was chilly dawn and she was sitting on Penny's deck, watching the sun rise. She'd made coffee for Patrick and Heather, who were still in bed, and was sipping hers from under a blanket in a comfy deck chair. They weren't leaving for a bit, and as far as she knew no one else was up yet, but she wanted to see the sun come up. Again. She'd seen a lot of sunsets from here at this point, but she couldn't get enough of them.

She should probably be exhausted—she'd spent the last few weeks on the trails with M&M tours every day. She'd met all kinds of people from all over the country—from Canada, from Europe…she was having a blast. All her rides since that first day had gone without any mishaps, too. Or at least without needing to call the EMTs. She'd gotten better at gauging ability for the downhill rides, and she loved the kids on the occasional flat rides along the river too. She felt like the Pied Piper or a mama duck or something, with all these little people following her on tiny wheels.

Her weekends—well, her weekday weekends—had been spent with Penny, here. She was out here a couple of evenings a week too, but she was trying to split her time carefully. She wanted to be a presence at the cabin and with the other guides because that was her job, and seasonal people stuck together. But she didn't think she'd be seasonal for long. It was nearly July and she was talking with the owners and with a bar in town about work beyond the summer.

And Penny had told her she should move in.

She smiled as the sky turned pink around the rim of the mountains, making the sky brighter but plunging the valley below into blue darkness. She'd never get bored of this. This mountain life was where she got her energy.

"Good morning."

Frankie jumped, startled out of her own head by Patrick, who pulled up a chair and joined her. "Good morning. Did I wake you up? I was trying to be quiet, but I needed coffee."

"Nope. I smelled the caffeine and I'm excited about our ride."

"Right? Me too. And I can't get enough of the sunrise."

"It can be pretty magical." Patrick sat with her and sipped his coffee.

They watched as the sun crested the mountain tops and the valley lit up again, bathed in pink and orange light. She could actually see the shadow moving across the treetops. "This is so beautiful."

"Isn't it? Growing up with this was amazing. I think Aspen thinks I don't appreciate it anymore, but I do. I just appreciate my sleep and my social life too. She's been a homebody until you moved out here." Patrick squinted at her. "Things have been good with you two, huh?"

"Things are great." She squinted back, playing. "She's it for me, Patrick."

Patrick's smile was almost as bright as the sunrise. "Excellent. Are you staying in Summit Springs?"

"One way or another. I'm trying to put together work and…"

"You can stay here. I mean, if Penny invites you, it's cool with me."

"She invited me." She laughed. "I was going to ask you, like all serious and shit. I was going to offer to help out and pay my share and whatever I needed to do to convince you to let me."

"I'm convinced." Patrick stuck his feet under her blanket. "And if you need work, Pines Peak hires winter seasonal too."

"I think M and M may have something for me but if they don't, can I hit you up for a recommendation?"

"Of course. Jesus, it's cold out here. July at dawn. Always chilly. I'm going to get dressed. Meet you in the kitchen at seven."

"See you then."

July at dawn may be chilly, but noon would be pretty warm. Depending on how crowded it was, they might be off the mountain before it got too hot, they were going early for a reason. She finished her last sip of coffee as the sun finished its show, a spectacularly bright-yellow sun rising over the peaks.

The ride up to the top of the double-diamond trail took over an hour. It wasn't hard, and it wasn't crowded, but it was full of switchbacks and long uphill stretches, and it took them a while. It was always a tradeoff—she could get up the mountain fast and call it a workout, but then she would be tired for the ride down, which was the whole reason she was making the climb. So she liked to take it easy on the way up. At the top, she and Patrick took a water break and they ran into a couple of other people headed their way, so they all sat and went over the terrain together.

"I've done this one twice," Patrick told them, going over the trail map. She listened carefully. The maps were helpful, but there was no substitute for someone that had ridden a course before. "This top section is the easiest. It's steep and it gets fast, though, so check your speed, especially if you feel like it's wet at all. When you hit the tree line…once you get about here," Patrick pointed to the map. "You get roots crossing and the pine branches are wicked. Duck through here. They fucking hurt if you don't have a face shield, and even if you do, you could get knocked off the bike."

"Been there," one of the riders said, shaking her head. "Thanks."

"Okay, so once you're past here, it's pretty sweet. There are wide branches and some installed features for getting across or around the creek beds, some natural turns and long, fast stretches…it's just fun as hell. Lots of room for tricks and air. And then toward the bottom here, this is a bunch of gnarly turns…you can tripod them, but make sure you're in control when you hit them, because it's one into another into another."

She loved listening to Patrick do this; he clearly loved it so much. He loved it like she did.

"Thanks, man."

"I'm Patrick. We'll let you go ahead and follow in a bit. There are some obvious pull-offs to catch your breath, and I'd use them. This is a long, awesome ride."

"Glad we ran into you. Thanks." The four riders nodded to each other, checked their gear, and took off. They'd obviously ridden together a lot, knew what order without discussing it and how much space to leave....They were experienced, which was good because Patrick made it sound like the terrain was no joke.

She couldn't wait.

"You lead?"

"Yeah, this first time. I'll show you the cool stuff."

"Right on." She sipped her water; then they gave their bikes a quick check while they waited for the other group to get ahead of them. Right before they left she texted Penny good morning, with a picture of the incredible view.

Frankie's number one rule about going up on the mountain? Check the weather first. Check the goddamn weather. This wasn't a hard concept—she did it reflexively from the parking lot every single time she rode.

And she had checked it this morning. She hadn't seen rain in the forecast until late in the day. They should have been fine.

They were just wrapping up a water break when they heard the thunder, and they turned to each other and stared like, *I thought we had this.*

"What is that?"

"I don't guess it's construction."

"No, I mean that." Patrick pointed to the sky where a black cloud was approaching. She could see the rain headed their way.

"Shit. I checked the weather. I swear to God."

"I did too. I did."

Damn mountain weather.

She puffed out a breath. "Okay, well…we better just head for the parking lot, huh?"

"Sounds like a plan."

They'd ride as far as they could and if worse came to worse, they'd walk their bikes. They weren't stupid.

They set off, and she could tell right away that Patrick was focused on getting off the trail. He didn't hit the tricks or go for air or any of the fun stuff. He stayed technical and wheels on the path.

They were headed into the final set of turns when the rain hit. They'd skipped the last pull-off to help make up time, but now they had to take it easy for safety, partly because they were riding into some fog and the visibility was starting to suck. She was close to Patrick, closer than she would be on a dry day, because she didn't want to lose sight of him, and she wanted to stay in hearing distance.

They took the first turn fine, and the second, and then a loud clap of thunder rocked the ground and echoed against the rocks. They instinctively slowed down even more, but the skies suddenly got scary dark and the heavens opened up. She was just about to suggest they get off their bikes when Patrick's wheel got stuck in something, maybe thick sand, maybe mud, and it slipped right out from under him. He and his bike went sideways, right over the backside of a turn.

"Patrick!"

Oh, fuck.

She dumped her bike and peered over the edge of the embankment, but she couldn't see him. She actually couldn't see where he'd gone.

"Patrick!"

Fuck. Okay. Think, Frankie.

Other people could be behind them on the trail. She needed to get out of the way, but there was nowhere to pull over, nowhere to park her bike at all—and even if there was, she probably wouldn't find it in this rain. She picked it up off the trail and wedged it between some tree branches high up on the edge of the bank, then peered over again.

"Patrick? Patrick!" she shouted one more time but got no answer. The rain was making it hard to see, but she thought she heard the click of a wheel spinning. "Patrick…"

She seriously couldn't see. And she couldn't be sure what would happen if she climbed over this rim…she could easily slide down there with him, especially with it being so wet. She didn't want to get stuck, but she couldn't just stand here either.

She pulled out her cell phone, hoping she could call the EMTs, and thanked all the powers she could think of that she seemed to have cell service.

"Summit Mountain Rescue." She could hear the voice on the line, but it was garbled. "What is the emergency?"

She took a breath and closed her eyes. Just the facts. Just like she'd been trained.

"Hey, this is Frankie Hoffman, I'm a guide with M and M. My friend Patrick Young and I are on the lower half of J-five ninety-eight in the hairpins and he's gone over the rim with his bike. It's pouring rain, I can't see shit, and he's not answering me."

"Hi, Frankie. My name is Gil. Did you say Patrick Young? You're breaking up a little. What trail did you say you were on? I'll dispatch someone now."

"J-five ninety-eight."

"Frankie, I got hairpins, but I…which trail—"

"Hello? J-five ninety-eight. The lower half of J-five ninety-eight." *Dammit.* She squinted into the storm. "I think I see his bike in a tree. Fuck. Patrick?" She shouted again, but still no response. "He's not answering me."

"Which trail…Frankie?"

Fuck. Gil couldn't hear her. She heard a branch crack and Patrick shouted.

"Shit, I hear him. Patrick!" *Oh, God.*

"Frankie!"

"I can't see you!"

"I'm stuck in a…in a fucking tree. Frankie? I just fell a few feet…my leg is…hurts. I need help…"

"I have to get to him."

"I think you should—" Whatever Gil said after that was garbled.

"Gil? I'm going to find a way around. Can you hear me? I'm making my way through these turns on foot."

"Fran—with the—" There was more static on the line. Gil was talking, but she couldn't make out what he was saying. There was water coming down through the hairpins now, turning it into a fucking waterslide, and she slipped in the mud a bunch of times before finding a way over and out of them.

"Patrick?"

"I'm…fuck. I'm here. I'm okay."

Uh-huh. What did "okay" mean? "I'm coming. Just…wait. Don't move!" She was shouting over the rain to be heard.

"Are you there? Gil? He's…I can see his bike so he must be —" She lost her footing and slid, put a hand out to catch herself and her phone went flying. "Fuck!"

"Frankie?" Oh, Patrick was close. "This is…oh, fuck. It fucking hurts."

"I dropped my phone," she called out. She was okay, just covered in mud and half-blind with the rain, but sure, she was just fine. She looked around but the water was rushing here and there and who the fuck knew where her phone could have gone.

She took a breath. Gil knew they were near the hairpins, right? He must have heard her. *Help is coming*, she told herself and went to be with Patrick.

"Frankie. I…see you." She could hear Patrick's hard breaths now.

She squinted into the weather and finally caught sight of

him. As it turned out, he was only about six feet from the ground. "I'm coming. Jesus. Where are you hurt?"

"Not sure. My leg is…at a really creative angle."

Oh, great.

"Okay, I'm here. I'm right below you, but don't move, you're…balanced somehow and…" She saw it clearly now. That leg was broken, maybe dislocated, definitely messed up. "I'm looking you over from here, I don't want to move you alone. The EMTs will find us." They would. They had to. Hopefully soon. In the meantime, she found some shelter from the rain under Patrick's tree and reached up to take his hand. He squeezed it hard. "I'm here. You're going to be okay." She tried to distract him. "The dispatcher, Gil, he seemed nice."

"Gil? Oh, he's a…he's a, um. He's a buddy of mine."

Shit, Patrick sounded like he might pass out. She was going to have to keep him talking.

"How do you know him?"

"We do ski patrol? In…in…in the winter. Fuck, I'm cold."

"Oh, yeah? Tell me about him." She checked for blood but didn't see any. Patrick's helmet was in place, and his hands looked a little raw maybe but not bloody.

"Oh, you…you want me to…to talk, huh? Good idea. Good. Okay."

"About Gil."

"Yes. He…skis like…like his ass is on fire."

Patrick kept talking, if slowly, and she kept watching him, but after a bit she started getting cold too. She was shivering and she knew he had to be worse. She had an emergency thermal blanket in her kit, but her supplies were all up with her bike and his were up in a tree. She wasn't sure it was safer for her to leave him, so for now at least, they were just going to have to tough it out.

"Cold," Patrick said. "I want to move. Can you get me down now? I'm getting...I can't...Frankie?"

"I'm here. I'm right here. Don't you move, I don't want you to fall. Help is coming, okay? They'll be—"

"Frankie?"

Oh, thank fuck.

"Over here!" She shouted back. "They're here. See? I told you. They're here. You're good." *Thank God.*

"Help!" Patrick shouted weakly. He was losing it a little, and who could blame him?

"We're coming."

She pushed the water out of her eyes and saw three people headed her way.

She waved, but her arm felt like it weighed a hundred pounds.

Jesus Christ, she was freezing.

CHAPTER 16

"Okay, he's in surgery, and the ER just released her."

"Surgery?" Aspen stood anxiously as Heather made her way back from the nurse's station. "They did? Where is she? I should go get her." She needed to get her hands on Frankie. See that she was okay. How was Heather so calm?

"They're bringing her up to us. You want some coffee?"

"Okay." She took a few steps toward the elevators to wait. "And Patrick? What are they saying? Why surgery?"

"He broke his leg in two places, so they're putting in pins and setting it. Depending on how it goes, he might need a second surgery, but otherwise he's fine."

Otherwise fine? How is that fine? "Second surgery?"

"Worst-case scenario. They're hoping not. He's in great shape, Aspen." Heather looked at her. "Really, he'll be fine. He's going to be pissed that his riding season is over, but he didn't hit his head, and they didn't find any other injuries."

"Had to hurt, though." Wasn't it okay to worry about her brother? About Frankie?

"Do you remember his skiing accident a few years ago? That was worse."

"He told me about it, but I was away at school. He didn't make it sound that bad…a couple of broken ribs, he said."

Heather grinned at her. "He had his head and neck in a halo."

"Jesus. He didn't tell me that."

"Because you're a wreck over a broken leg." Heather handed her a paper cup filled with hot, black coffee.

"Broken and needing surgery." Was Heather crazy? "And you're not worried. You're not upset at all?"

"I was when you called me, of course. I was worried until the doctor said it was his leg and that was it. I want to see him, sure. But Patrick…he plays hard. He always has. He and Frankie were up on a double-black, that's as tough a trail as they get."

A double-black? She assumed the trails were marked like ski trails, so yeah, that was a serious ride. All she'd known was the trail number, and thank God for that. Patrick had texted it to her before their ride. "She didn't tell me it was such a tough hill." She should have assumed, though. They were both experienced. She was starting to see a pattern here.

"And can you blame her?" Heather winked at her, and she grinned sheepishly.

"Okay, okay. Shut up."

"I can walk now, she's right there." Frankie's voice came down the hall.

"Frankie?" She rushed over, trying not to spill her coffee. "Oh my God, why are you in a wheelchair? What's wrong?"

"Nothing is wrong, I'm fine."

The orderly stopped the chair and Frankie stood. She looked a little tired and very muddy, but she did seem okay. "Just rules," he said.

Frankie rolled her eyes.

She nodded to the orderly. "Well, thank you."

"You're welcome. Have a good day." He winked at her and left.

"How is Patrick?"

She gave Frankie a one-armed hug and Frankie hugged her back. "He's in surgery."

"It's just his leg."

"Ah. Okay." Frankie nodded like that was just fine.

Totally fine.

Everyone was fine.

Ugh.

"You good, Heather?" Frankie asked.

Heather nodded. "I'm okay. You're filthy."

"So much mud." Frankie grinned.

"Patrick usually checks the weather. I'm so sorry."

Frankie shook her head. "He did. I did too. Even the EMTs said the storm came up quickly. Patrick got caught in some mud or something on a hairpin, and when he stuck his foot out for balance, his rear wheel slid out from under him. We weren't even moving that fast. Really, we were being super careful. The timing was crazy, though, I was just about to suggest we walk the rest of the way."

She didn't want to hear this story, did she? "He went over a bank?" Just that much was making her cringe.

"Yeah. His momentum just took him right over."

"And then what?" Unlike Aspen, Heather looked like she was ready for a good story.

"Him, his bike, just...*whoop*! It was crazy. And then the rain was coming down so hard, and I called the EMTs because I couldn't see shit, and I wasn't going to be able to get him off the mountain alone. This guy, Gil, picked up. Patrick said he was a friend."

"Gil Gray? Sure. They're on ski patrol together. He's built like a mountain himself."

"Yeah, Patrick said. But we didn't talk long, the cell service was bad. I wasn't sure he heard me."

"He didn't." Aspen interrupted, shaking her head. "But he heard Patrick's name and he called me."

"Oh, shit." Frankie went a little white. "God, I'm...wow. I'm glad he got Patrick's name. It was cold as fuck up there and...I was worried, to be honest."

"I was worried too."

"Hey." Frankie hugged Aspen again. "God, I'm sorry. I didn't realize. I'm okay."

Heather rubbed Frankie's arm. "They found you. Patrick will be okay too."

"Yeah. Okay." Frankie leaned closer to Heather. "He got stuck in a tree, you know."

"In a tree?" Heather's eyes went wide.

"In a fucking tree." Frankie chuckled. "Fortunately, it caught him. But he'd also fallen a few feet, and it's hard to know, but I think that fall is what broke his leg. At least he was lower down, though. The EMTs could reach him without a ladder."

How was this story funny? Her brother had been stuck in a tree. And not on purpose. "Jesus Christ." Aspen paced away. She didn't have the stomach for this.

"She's been very worried," she heard Heather say, quietly.

"Mrs. Young?"

Aspen turned reflexively but stopped herself. Heather hesitated, but Frankie nudged her. "Oh! That's me. Man, I am still getting used to the 'Mrs.' thing. Newlyweds. Sorry."

"Oh, congratulations. I wanted to give you a quick update. The surgery went well; they're just finishing up with him now. We'll come to get you in a bit so you can see him in recovery. Okay?"

"Yes. There's family—"

"Only you can see him in recovery. They can see him when we get him to his room."

"Okay. Great. Thank you."

The doctor left, and Aspen sat with her coffee.

"Hey, are you okay?" Frankie sat with her and rested a hand on her back.

"It's weird not being the next of kin anymore."

"Little brother has a wife." Frankie smiled.

"Yeah. You're okay, though? You're sure?"

"I'm fine. I didn't fall or anything, I was just wet and really cold. They put a heating blanket on me and got me some coffee and then let me go. There wasn't even time for me to ask for a visitor."

"I was worried. I'm still worried." She shook her head, talking quietly so Heather didn't overhear. "Heather made it sound like worrying was stupid, but...well, I'm sorry, I worry. It's not stupid, it's me."

"It's not stupid, baby." Frankie's arms circled her and she held on, not caring about the mud. She needed the hug and the reassurance. Frankie felt solid, whole, just fine, and she took a breath, trying to let some of the tension go.

"I was worried too for a while. I mean, I had him, and I was right there, but I could barely see in the rain. I'm trained and could have helped him, but I was afraid I'd do more harm than good if I moved him. He was talking, though, mostly awake. He seemed to know what was going on. I mean, after I lost my stupid cell phone I was pretty worried, but they know what they're doing up there."

"The dispatcher said you did everything right. Using your names and...so he found me." She let go, leaning back to get a look at Frankie. "You were on a double-black diamond."

"Yeah." Frankie shrugged. "It's a gnarly trail. Fun as hell. Hard."

"I will never not worry, you know. I want you to have your fun, but—"

Frankie winked at her. "Okay. So, I'll only tell you what you need to know."

She snorted. "Gee, thanks."

"I'm going to ride. So is he, as soon as he can. And hundreds of other people this summer. We love it." Frankie shrugged.

"It's so dangerous, though."

"It's not. There's risk, sure. But I don't do it for the risk. I'm not like that. I do it for the challenge and I'm as careful as I can be, but accidents happen. Maybe even to me. I can't not go have fun."

It didn't matter that Frankie was right. She was still going to worry. Summit Springs was an adventure kind of place, an athletic place, and people were out doing all kinds of things, all of which had some element of risk. That was the nature of where she lived. It just wasn't her world. Hers was the other half—the arts, the quiet of nature, the slower side of town.

She stood and paced a few steps away, sipped her coffee, and looked out the window. She could barely see the mountain her brother and Frankie had just been hauled off—the top was shrouded in heavy rain clouds and the sky was a dark gray.

"The sun will be out in a couple of hours." Frankie was next to her again, eyes focused out the window too.

"Is that a metaphor?"

"Well, I was a lit major." Frankie chuckled.

"Thanks for taking care of him."

"I didn't do much. I just watched him hang out in a tree for a while and kept him talking."

"His leg is broken in two places, he might need another surgery, but Heather says he's going to be okay." She took a breath and puffed it out. Saying all of that out loud helped a little, made it sink in that he was alive and mostly okay.

"Yeah, I knew about the broken leg. I was more concerned about other things, but I guess he was lucky that tree was there."

The doctor came to get Heather. She and Frankie waited for another hour or so; then Heather came back to get them.

"Aspen? He's awake. You two want to see him?" Heather called from down the hall.

"Yes, please." She got up from her seat where she'd been leaning on Frankie and hurried to Heather. Frankie followed right behind her.

The head of Patrick's bed was raised a little, and his leg was elevated, but he was smiling when they got there. "Hey, sis."

"Patrick." She went right to him and hugged him and he hugged her too, nice and tight like always. "Are you okay? Does it hurt?"

"Not right now, they have me doped up. I'll probably pass out in a minute."

Now that he mentioned it, she could see the dopey look in his eyes. "You're supposed to ride your bike, or climb trees. Not both at the same time."

That made everyone laugh, and the tension in the room eased a little.

"Oh. Damn. Why didn't someone tell me that before I rode today?"

"My bad." Frankie put out a hand and she and Patrick exchanged some complicated fist-bump, handshake, bro-hug thing that made Aspen smile. She hadn't known they had that between them. It was sweet.

"Dude. Where's my bike?"

"Still in a tree. No worries, though. Mountain patrol said they'd pick them up when the rain clears. I'll go grab them

tomorrow after work and take them over to Scratchin'
Gravel for a tune-up."

"Oh. Right on. Thanks, bro."

Frankie nodded. "You got it."

Patrick's eyes closed for a second, but he blinked them
open. "Heather says you're worried. I'm good. This will heal
up long before ski patrol starts. But I'm going to be a pain in
the ass at the house." She got a big grin, and Patrick squeezed
her fingers.

"Oh, great. You were already a mooch to begin with." She
leaned over and kissed his cheek. "I love you, you idiot."

"I know. I love you too. I'll make it up to you. I'll make
Heather cook more."

Heather's eyebrow shot up. "Oh? And Mr. Stuck At Home
can order Instacart and run a Swiffer around the house with
the best of them."

"Yeah." Patrick chuckled and his eyes closed again. This
time, they stayed closed.

She put his hand down and gave it a pat. "I'm going to
take Frankie home and put her filthy self in a shower. You
want me to bring you back dinner?"

"That would be great. Would you be willing to pick up a
burger from Whitewater for him? Maybe a Caesar salad
for me?"

"Of course. I'll take Frankie for dinner, and then I'll
come by."

"Thank you so much."

"I'll bring him some real undies too." She gave Heather a
hug. "Just call or text if you need anything else."

"A shower sounds like heaven," Frankie said as they left
the room. "You okay?"

Aspen shook her head. "Everyone is so worried about me,
and I'm not the one that got hurt."

"Well, we love you. Deal with it." Frankie bumped shoulders with her, and she hugged Frankie's waist as they waited for the elevator.

"I was just thinking the same thing." She was going to worry. They could just deal with that too. "That, and you smell *really* bad."

Frankie glanced at her sharply. They were still laughing as the elevator doors closed.

CHAPTER 17

"*My* brain hurts."

Penny chuckled. "I know. I'd like to say we're almost done, but…"

Frankie rubbed her forehead, frowning at the pile of auction catalogs that Heather had just started folding.

"I just put on a pot of coffee, and I figure we can have a cocktail with lunch." Heather winked at them.

"There you go, Frankie. That's something to look forward to." Penny just stared at her laptop.

"What's for lunch?" Patrick called from the living room.

"Sandwiches," Heather answered. "Turkey or ham."

"Cool. Thanks. Hey, babe?"

Heather grinned and shook her head. "Yes?"

"Could you bring me the remote? I can't reach it."

Heather looked at them and rolled her eyes, then headed for the living room. "Sure thing."

"He's really milking that whole cast thing, huh?"

Penny chuckled. "You have no idea."

Frankie went back to proofing the auction bid sheets. The whole auction system was way more complicated than she'd realized. They had to get special tracking software and the sheets all had bar codes and numbers that had to match the items. She was going over the sheets to make sure everything was titled correctly and attributed to the right artists, checking them against a list that Penny had printed for her.

It was tedious, but it had to be done. Penny was stressed and wanted everything to be just right. Frankie definitely didn't want to be the one that made a mistake.

No pressure.

She'd picked up the auction catalogs yesterday, and everyone had held their breaths while Penny proofed them. It had taken her forever. If they'd actually been not breathing, they'd have all passed out. Patrick had even had both fingers crossed in the air the whole time. When Penny put it down and said the catalogs looked great, they'd all cheered like they were at a soccer game.

Halle-fucking-lujah.

Frankie had tried folding one this morning and it came out crooked, so she was immediately fired from that job and Heather took over. That was how stressed Penny was.

"Okay. Back to work." Heather reported to her spot. "I hear the ticket sales are going well?"

"Mhm." Penny's eyes were still glued to her screen. "Don't talk about it, it makes me nervous."

"Gotcha. Um. How's work, Frankie?"

That was wise; take the spotlight off Penny. "I love it. I expected it to be fun, but I've learned so much about people and about my sport. I thought I knew a lot, but I really think I learn something new every day."

"Weird that the summer is ending already, huh? I've got a teacher meeting next week and we start school the week after that."

"In August?"

"That's the schedule out here. I've heard the East Coast often starts later, but we're always that week."

"Wow. Cool. Are you excited?"

"I think so?" Heather smiled and looked thoughtful for a second. "It always takes me a few days to gear up, but I'm getting there. I'm excited to see the kids for sure."

"What grade do you teach?"

"Hey, babe?" Patrick called. "Would you mind bringing me a Coke?"

"Third grade." Heather sighed. "It would be wrong to kill him, right?"

"Probably."

"Dammit." Heather chuckled. "Let him wait a minute."

Frankie shook her head, watching Penny. "Are you doing okay?"

"Yeah. I'm just...anxious. This is important to me. I know I'm driving everyone crazy, I appreciate that you're putting up with me."

She took Penny's hand and squeezed it. "Of course. I'm all in, baby. This is going to be an amazing party, and you're going to rock it. It's a big deal, no wonder you're stressed. Anyone would be."

Not everyone was quite the control freak that Penny was, though.

She went to check on the coffee, poured everyone a cup, and brought them back to the table.

"Hey, guys." Patrick was suddenly there, on his crutches. In his defense, he looked pretty tired.

"You're up. How are you doing, man? You look like you're not sleeping." He seemed better than he had at the hospital for sure.

"Yeah. Just a little at a time. It hurts at night. Doc says that will get better." Patrick was not the patient type. He looked completely miserable.

"That sucks."

"I got a job. They just called."

"A job? With a broken leg?" Heather sounded incredulous.

"Yep. I told the folks at Pines Peak what was up with my leg and they have a desk job for me to get me through until I can get on the mountain again. Reservations and booking, they said. I don't even care, it's a job, right?"

Heather got up and hugged him. "That's amazing, baby."

"I don't want to be totally worthless, you know?"

"You're not worthless, you've been working."

"Yeah, but I can't do the odd jobs and day-work stuff with this leg. I figured I'd call, and it worked out."

"You never know, this could be something you can keep when you're not doing patrol," Penny suggested. "Congrats, Patrick."

"Sit, baby. I'll get your Coke."

Heather got Patrick settled with them at the table. It turned out even Patrick was better at folding those brochures than she was. They were quiet for a while, each of them concentrating, so they all jumped when Frankie's phone rang.

"Huh. It's work." M&M was calling on a Monday. That couldn't be good, could it? Frankie answered it quickly. "Hello?"

"Frankie? It's Liz at M and M. I'm sorry to bother you on your day off."

"Hi, Liz. That's no problem. Is everything okay?"

"Oh, yes. I was calling about your request for winter work."

"Yeah?" She really hoped this was good news. She just needed something—anything—to do. And she wanted to bike with them again next summer.

"I wanted to let you know that we will find a place for you this winter if you still want to stay on. We need someone part-time in the office for sure, so I can start you there at least, and we'll see how things go. It's just day-to-day office work, but I was thinking you could keep your eyes open over the winter season and see what else might interest you. Then I could help place you somewhere more your speed next winter. Work for you?"

She glanced up at Penny, who was watching her now instead of the laptop, and gave her a thumbs-up. "That sounds great. I appreciate it. Thank you so much."

"And I hope you'll stay on with us into next summer again?"

Yes. Yes yes yes! "I would like that. Yes, please. This has been a great experience."

"We've got nothing but good reviews for both you and the new biking program. I'd like to schedule a meeting in a couple of weeks to talk about what we can do next year."

"Sounds good. Thank you."

"Listen, you have a—oh. One more question. For the winter, will you need housing?"

"Uh..." *Oh, shit.* She didn't think so but... "Will I need winter housing?" she repeated, but she was really asking Penny.

Penny shook her head and mouthed, *No, stay here*, finger-pointing downward emphatically. Frankie checked in with Heather and Patrick, who were both nodding as well. Patrick gave her a wink and a thumbs-up.

"Yes. Sorry, am I breaking up?"

"No, I've got you. Thanks, I won't need housing. I'm good." So good. Amazing, as a matter of fact.

"Great. Well, you'll be glad for that Subaru when the snow hits."

"I know I will. Listen, thanks again, Liz. I appreciate it."

"You're welcome. Enjoy your days off, see you Wednesday."

"Yep. Bye-bye." She hung up, but she couldn't stop smiling. "I'm really staying." She would have stayed in any case, but knowing she had some work was good. Knowing M&M wanted her back riding in the summer was better.

"I was going to insist anyway, you know."

She leaned in and kissed Penny's cheek. "I know. I just…I wanted to know I had work." That was important to her. "I have two nights a week bartending at Whitewater if I want them, so I'm going to take those too. Weekends. Good money."

"Congrats, Frankie." Heather clinked coffee mugs with her.

"Perfect." Penny's voice sounded more happy than stressed.

"It is perfect. And you're all sure you're okay with me living here? With all the chaos?" She was very used to roommates, she'd always had them, and Patrick and Heather were great people.

Patrick laughed. "You'll keep Aspen out of my hair."

"Ha." Penny took her hand and kissed her fingers. "I want you here. Period. You'll make the chaos better."

She squeezed Penny's hand, feeling whole for the first time in a long time. "You want some lunch? I could use a break."

"Oh, good idea." Penny stood, stretching.

Heather smiled at her. "It'll be fun having you here."

It would be the most fun ever. Living here with Penny in this amazing house with that amazing view and what was basically her new family? Frankie couldn't think of anything better. It was everything she'd wanted. Everything she'd come out here for.

More than everything, really.

CHAPTER 18

The blue dress with the slightly sexy open back or the basic little black dress that went well with every occasion? Frankie stood in the center of the bunkhouse bedroom, trying to decide between the two dresses that were hanging on the bunk bed, feeling ridiculously insecure.

Truth be told, she didn't care much for dresses, but she couldn't wear jeans to a gala—especially not Penny's gala—and that was literally her only other choice. She'd brought the black dress from Vermont, she'd worn it a bunch of times, and she was comfortable in it. The blue one she'd bought at a store in town last week with Lucy, because all her bunkmates had told her that basic black was for funerals and she needed something special for her girlfriend's gala.

"What are you doing?" Lucy breezed by her, took the black dress off the bunk where it was hanging and hung it up on an exposed closet rack by the bunkroom door. "No."

She sighed. "This is so…"

"Hot? Yep, it is. It looks great on you."

"It feels like too much."

"This is a black-tie optional gala, Frankie. That dress is absolutely appropriate."

She'd never been to anything black-tie optional. She wasn't even sure what that meant. She took a breath and pulled the dress down off the hanger.

"People! We're going to be late." Alex called from the kitchen.

"Put it on, Frankie."

"Right." She pulled the dress on and Lucy fastened the back, then she slipped into her low-heeled black sandals—those had also come from Vermont but had been roommate approved—and scanned the room. "There's no mirror."

Alex had done her hair and although Frankie hated makeup, Lucy had convinced her to try a little and had helped her with some mascara and a little liner around her eyes.

"Frankie, you look great."

"I need to see, though." God, she was so nervous. Dressing up like this was a very rare thing for her.

"Uh...oh. Okay, hang on, I got this." Lucy moved away and took a picture with her cell phone. "Here."

Frankie took the phone and scrutinized the picture, hardly recognizing herself. "Wow." She looked...good. The dress was kind of hot, even. And her hair had a little bit of a wave and flowed over her shoulders. She nodded, smiling slightly. "I might pass for a grown-up."

"See?" Lucy took her phone back. "That is how you impress your VIP girlfriend at her gala."

"I don't need to impress her, though, I just want to support her."

"Shut. Up." Lucy grinned.

"Lucy? Bring her." Alex sounded impatient now.

"We're coming."

Frankie took a breath and followed Lucy out into the

kitchen, grateful that no one had argued with her about the sandals. She was not a heels person.

"Oh my God, look at you. You are gorgeous. Turn, turn…" Milo took a couple of steps away to admire, making her blush.

"Are you serious?"

Milo rolled his eyes. "Turn, woman. I want to see the whole thing."

She did a little spin, both embarrassed and excited by the attention.

Alex gave her a deep nod. "Oh, girl. You are *hot*."

"Thank you. Now stop making me blush. You both look absolutely incredible."

Milo was so handsome in his simple gray suit and long, black tie, and Alex was practically a show-stopper in a colorful jumpsuit.

"Oh, thank you." Milo posed like he was on the red carpet. Alex looped an arm through Milo's and blew kisses to her. She and Lucy applauded.

"You are too much."

Okay. It was time to get it together. If her friends could do this—put a night aside for her and dress up—if Milo, of all people, could put on an actual tie to support her on an important night, she could totally get on board. This was going to be fun.

"Are we ready?"

Alex's smile was as stunning as their outfit. "Yes, please. I want champagne." Alex took her arm this time which was hilarious because they were at least a foot taller.

"And you will have it." She straightened her shoulders and tried to be gallant, opening the cabin door for everyone.

"To the Milo-mobile!" They all piled into Milo's Jeep— they weren't taking her car because she planned to ride home with Penny. It wasn't the easiest car to get into in her dress, though, and they all laughed as she flashed half of M&M even with Milo's help.

Milo started the car. "You know, I didn't even ask where we were going."

"Do you know Cedar Ranch?"

"Oh, yeah. That place is gorgeous."

"Wait we're going up to Cedar?" Alex seemed so on board with this adventure. "Oh, wow."

"What happened to having it at Penny's place?"

"That got scrapped early on. It's a hell of a drive out there, for one thing. I mean, I wouldn't want to drive it after a glass or two of wine, you know? But they had to rethink it because Penny got so much interest as she was talking with people that there just wouldn't have been enough room for everyone at the house. Cedar is owned by friends of the woman that founded the co-op, and she discovered they had an open Sunday night and negotiated some amazing rate. Like half price. So, they jumped on it."

"That's so cool. How many people are coming?"

"Are you sitting down?" She grinned because of course they were. "Penny said they sold over three hundred tickets."

"Oh, my God. Really? So, this is a huge party."

"It is. It's mostly locals, but apparently the resort sold a bunch of tickets too and is providing transportation for their guests." Penny had been proud of that; working together with the resort had become an important goal.

The drive to Cedar Ranch was so much fun that the gala was going to have to work hard to catch up. The venue didn't disappoint, though—from the second they drove onto the property, it felt like a celebration. There were balloons on the gate and along the drive, and the big barn's wide-open doors were warm and welcoming.

They parked, and Frankie noticed as they approached the party barn that everyone had kind of fallen in behind her, so she tried to look like someone that should be at a big important gala and not a schlump of a mountain biking instructor.

In Summit Springs, however, people respected what she did for a living in a way they didn't in other places.

"Oh, my God." Alex's voice was full of awe as they all walked in, and they were right. It was hard to believe this huge, open room had ever been a barn. The room had high-top tables all along the center aisle and string lights hung across the venue making it feel romantic, like the place was full of stars. And of course, all kinds of art lined the walls.

"Hey, it's a birdbath. Oh, I have to go see." Alex went right over with Milo.

Lucy popped up next to her. "This is so beautiful. Are you okay if we go have a look around?"

"Oh, yeah. Of course. I think I see a bar over there too."

"Good eye, girl. Go find your woman."

"That's exactly what I'm going to do." Once she finished just taking in this amazing vibe. Everyone was dressed up, socializing and laughing at some of the tables or slowly moving by the art exhibits. There was a band playing at the far end, and she thought she saw Minnie with them so she headed that way.

"Frankie?" Minnie saw her first and crossed the empty dance floor. "Oh, thank God you're here."

"Hey, Minnie." Her smile faded as Minnie got closer. "What's wrong?"

"Aspen is a wreck. Go out the back." Minnie pointed to a set of curtains that hid the far wall of the room. "There's a little building across the way, she's there, getting ready."

What? What could possibly be wrong? "Getting ready? Hasn't the party already started?"

"I know. I had to come out here to warm up, but when I left Damon was there. Roz is playing hostess for now."

Oh, boy. She took a breath. "Okay. I'll find her, thanks."

Everything was perfect. The guests were arriving, Minnie was heading up the band, all the art was here....Frankie couldn't imagine what was wrong. She went through the curtains and the back doors, and found what had to be the building Minnie was talking about.

"Aspen?" she called as she went in.

Damon answered. "Over here, Frankie."

She followed the voice and found Aspen pacing and Damon looking like he was going to pull out his hair. "Penny?"

"She's been pacing..."

"Damon, get her a shot of something. Whiskey."

"Oh, that's a good idea. Why didn't I think of that?" Damon took off at a run.

"Penny?"

"You're late."

"A little. I'm sorry." She'd worked today and come off the mountain as soon as she could. "It was a longer drive than I thought it would be, and I had to...never mind."

Her excuses didn't matter right now. This couldn't possibly be about her.

"Why aren't you out there?" Penny turned to face her and Frankie sucked in a sharp breath. Holy crap, Penny was stunning.

"Do you know who is out there? Do you know how much money we've already raised? I don't even know what to say to these people. It's too much, I'm...I have to make a speech, and I'm speechless."

She just shook her head. "You are so beautiful."

Penny stared at her a second, then breathed in deep and hugged her.

"Oh. Hey. You're okay." She wrapped her arms around Penny and held on. "Everything is amazing. Minnie is about to sing, and people are smiling...the crew I brought got sucked right into the auction. You did it, Penny."

Penny sighed against her and her arms eased up.

"Sit, baby." She got Penny into a chair just as Damon came running in with a glass in his hand.

"Frankie, someone's bid almost four hundred on my birdbath, and we're just getting started." Damon handed her the whiskey.

"Wow, that's amazing. What would you have priced it in the gallery?"

"Two-seventy-five," Penny answered softly. Her voice sounded far away, awed. "And I'd have let someone bid me down to two-fifty."

"People are here to spend money, baby." She handed Penny the glass. "Drink that."

Damon watched her, worried. "Is she—"

"She's good. She'll be out in a minute. You go have fun."

"This is so cool. What a great idea, Aspen." Damon kissed Penny's cheek and hurried out.

When Frankie looked back, the glass was empty, and Frankie set it aside. "Good girl."

"The mayor is going to be here. The sheriff. Friends from town, friends of my parents'..."

"And they're going to have a good time, spend some money, and be proud of you."

Penny frowned at her. "You think so?"

Frankie's eyes went wide. "Penny. I'm proud of you, and I've only been in Summit Springs since June." It was hard to believe the summer would be over soon. "Those people know you as part of their community. Of course they're proud of you. And if you ask me, it looks like most people are planning on taking home some pottery, and the little cocktail wieners haven't even been passed yet."

Penny chuckled, her laugh breathy but genuine. Then she took another breath. "I hate whiskey."

"I know. Think of it like cough medicine. It'll get the job done." She liked it, but Penny never had. Tequila was another story, but it wasn't quite the same slap in the face. "Can you stand up?"

"Mhm." Penny stood, and Frankie futzed with her dress, straightening it out even where it didn't need it just to keep Penny focused. "Your dress is gorgeous. You're the most beautiful woman I've ever seen."

Penny's hazel eyes were shining. "Oh, Frankie. That's bullshit, but I love you for saying it."

"Yeah?" She held Penny's gaze, absolutely steady, and Penny smiled at her, nodding slowly. "I love you too."

Penny's kiss tasted like whiskey and felt like the truth, and she leaned right into it. She knew for sure, no matter what, she was staying right here. She was useful, she'd make herself invaluable at M&M year-round. There wouldn't be any more time or miles between them.

Penny pulled back just slightly, lips still so close to hers. "I guess I'd better get out there."

"You're the star of this show, baby."

Penny gave her another peck on the lips, then looked around. "That doesn't make me any less nervous. I had a little shawl…"

"Right here." Frankie picked it up and draped it over her shoulders.

"My face?"

"It's still there."

Penny poked her and groaned. "Do I have raccoon eyes?"

"No." She laughed. "Your mascara is firmly in place." She offered Penny her arm.

"Thank you for coming, Frankie."

"Are you kidding? How could I not be at the biggest event in Summit Springs all summer?"

～

The biggest event in Summit Springs all summer.

That probably wasn't true. The town was busy in the summer with festivals that brought people to town to have fun, hear musicians and try all kinds of food. There were big weddings, of course, and the resort always had something going on for its guests.

But this was big. Aspen's little committee had sold three hundred tickets, and there were more to be had at the door. They'd given up on the idea of a sit-down meal very early on and instead had passed hors d'oeuvres and a buffet table with finger food. There was a cash bar for alcohol. There was great lighting and good music, and people were all dressed up. Even Frankie.

Oh, God. She hadn't told Frankie how beautiful she was in that incredible dress.

Aspen glanced around quickly, hoping to catch Frankie's eye, which she did, but only just in time to be handed a microphone. "The stage is yours."

"I hate stages."

"You've got this, Aspen." Minnie leaned close and held her gaze like she was giving a pep talk to a football team. "You *own* that stage, woman. This is the place to be. Tell everybody thank you for paying crazy prices to come to your party. That's how cool you are."

She nodded. They had paid. She hadn't begged anyone to buy a ticket, they'd been an easy sell. She stepped up onto the stage and the band went quiet. The lights even dimmed slightly and the room settled as people turned toward the stage. Toward her.

And Frankie was right in front, dead center, watching along with a handful of her artists.

She took a breath. "Good evening, everyone."

The room went completely quiet then. She was moderately terrified now, so she did the only thing she could think of to do. She smiled. "Welcome to what I hope will be the first annual summer gala in support of Pure Art Collective."

There was applause—started by the artists she thought—and it carried through the room. She went on. "Like many of your own businesses, we had a tough winter. In recent weeks, the management at Pines Peak has shown a lot of interest in bringing local culture to their guests. I want to thank them and their amazing staff for their willingness to work with all of us and for keeping their ties with the community as strong as ever.

"We're all adapting. I am sure many of you know what we at Pure have gone through as we evaluated how viable our gallery was, how realistic it would be to stay in business." She looked around the room at all the nods and knew she was in good company. "The artists in our collective are brilliant, talented people who are inspired by Summit Springs. That's why we're here. The landscape, the mountain air, the sunshine, all make for good art, but those things alone can be found in other places. The people of this community—all of you—are why we stay. You're why I came home from college in Vermont—another beautiful mountain landscape—to start my dream of running an art gallery here in Summit Springs.

"In the months leading up to this event we've had help with our rent, help buying supplies, help finding new outlets to sell our work. The help came from this community, so this party—this gala—is not just a fund raiser, though certainly we do need that. It's also for you, our friends and neighbors, to come together and celebrate creativity, our vibrant and beautiful town, and each other. I will be back later to give you an update on how the auctions are going and properly thank the long list of people without whom this evening would not be happening, but for now, I can tell you that tickets sales have far exceeded our expectations, and the support from all of you has also far exceeded our hopes. It's going to be an amazing night.

"Thank you all for coming. Have a drink, go see and feel the love our artists put into their work, and have fun!"

The applause was loud and happy, and as the lights came up, she saw the movement in the crowd shift from milling around the tables to lingering near the edges of the room where the bidding was happening.

"That was great! You were really good." Minnie took her mic and the band began to vamp. "You did your job, I'm going to do mine now. Go have some fun."

"Thank you." The adrenaline rush as her nerves subsided was crazy. She rested a hand on the railing as she climbed down from the little stage, and realized it was trembling slightly.

Frankie ran over and hugged her as soon as she stepped off the stairs. "You were so good. That was perfect."

She hugged Frankie too. "I didn't tell you how beautiful you are tonight."

"Oh." That sweet, shy smile was strange on Frankie. And lovely. She didn't see that look very often. "Thank you. I…it's a story. You know me and dresses. It's a love-hate kind of relationship."

"Well, I love this one." She took Frankie's hand.

Frankie blushed. "How about we start with a drink?"

She laughed as she walked with Frankie to the bar. "Didn't I already start with that shot of whiskey?"

"Yep. A little liquid courage, I've heard people call it."

"It worked. I was a wreck."

"Aspen." She looked toward the voice, and there was Bucky, headed her way.

With the mayor.

"I want you to meet someone."

"Hey, baby."

"Oh, thank you." Aspen never made it to the bar, but Frankie would occasionally excuse herself, and somehow, she always had a glass of wine in her hand. She took this one from Frankie, thinking it would probably be her last. The auction had closed half an hour ago. Damon had collected all the bidding sheets, and he and a handful of volunteers were busy matching bidding numbers to items and collecting payment at the computers up front. Thank goodness he was more tech-savvy than she was.

"We should let you go. This was a fantastic party." Jed Brightlow had stopped her on his way out the door. "I was a little worried at the beginning of that speech."

She chuckled. "The town has always had a give-and-take relationship with the resort. I remember some of it growing up because so many of us worked up there and it just kept getting bigger. But this isn't a resort town; it's so much more than that. We just want to keep it that way. You've been a big help. Thank you."

Jed shook her hand. "I'll see you Tuesday. Hopefully you still have some pieces to bring up to us; it seems like every-thing here got good bids."

"We have plenty, don't you worry." They'd been very deliberate in putting aside work for the various gift shops. All of her artists would be represented. "Good night."

She took a sip of her wine as they walked away; then Frankie took it back from her. "The night isn't quite over."

"No, I know. I have so much cleanup to do. And I have to organize delivery of the items people couldn't take with them, and—"

"Later. I'll help with all of that. But the band is still playing, and I haven't had a chance to ask you to dance."

She smiled. Frankie had been right by her side, not just looking pretty and making small talk, but actually being her partner, supporting her through the evening as she met nearly everyone in the room. "So, ask."

Frankie laughed. "Aspen Young, will you dance with me?"

"I would love to. And you can call me Penny."

ABOUT JODI

JODI takes herself way too seriously and has been known to randomly break out in song. Her characters are imperfect but genuine, stubborn but likable, often kinky, and frequently their own worst enemies. They are characters you can't help but fall in love with while they stumble along the path to their happily ever after. For those looking to get on her good side, Jodi's addictions include nonfat lattes, Malbec and tequila any way you pour it.

Website: jodipayne.net
Newsletter: https://readerlinks.com/l/2317334
All Jodi's Social Links: linktr.ee/jodipayne

A NOTE FROM THE AUTHOR

Hey there!

I just wanted to take a minute to say thank you for taking the time to read Top of the World. I hope you enjoyed it. I know everyone is busy and our TBR (to be read) lists are out of control, so it means a lot to me that I ended up at the top of your pile this time.

If you have a moment, please consider leaving a review. All honest reviews are much appreciated.

If you're looking for more of my work, why not join my newsletter? Just go here: https://readerlinks.com/l/2317334.

WANT MORE SUMMIT SPRINGS BOOKS?

Check out the other books in the series!

*I*nterested in learning more about my books? Want free fiction and news? Join my newsletter!

What's Up with Jodi
https://readerlinks.com/l/2317334

MORE BOOKS BY JODI

Sapphic Romance
Summit Springs Novels
Top of the World,
Christmas Bizarre, with BA Tortuga

Best Lesbian Love Stories, Summer Flings
Sapphic Planet

M/M Romance
Mergers & Acquisitions
Stable Hill (MMM)
Not Over You: A Sons of Cape Cod Novel
Soft Limits: A Deviations Novel
Creative Process
Linchpin
Whence He Came

With BA Tortuga
Les's Bar Series
Just Dex
Hide Bound

The Triskelion Series
Breaking the Rules
Making a Mark (MM/MM)
Making the Rules (MMMM)